Elizabeth Bowen's
Irish Stories

POOLBEG PRESS: DUBLIN

First published 1978 by
Poolbeg Press Ltd.,
Knocksedan House,
Swords, Co. Dublin, Ireland.

This selection is published by arrangement with Jonathan Cape Limited.
Individual stories copyright in 1930, 1934, 1940, 1941, 1944, 1949, 1952,
1956. "Sunday Afternoon" first appeared in *Life & Letters* (ND); "The
Tommy Crans" in *The Cat Jumps* (1934); "Her Table Spread" in the
Broadsheet Press (1930); "A Love Story" in *Horizon* (1940);
"Unwelcome Idea" and "Summer Night" in *Look At All Those Roses*
(1941); "A Day in the Dark" in *Botteghe Oscure* (1956); "Hand in
Glove" in *The Second Ghost Book* (Barrie and Rockliffe, 1952); "The
Happy Autumn Fields" in *The Cornhill Magazine* (1944).

The generous assistance of An Comhairle Ealaion (The Arts Council)
in the publication of this book is gratefully acknowledged.

Designed by Steven Hope

The kind permission of Finlay Colley Esq. for the use of the portrait of
Elizabeth Bowen by G. M. B. Holland in 1924 is acknowledged with
thanks.

Printed by Cahill Printers Limited,
East Wall Road, Dublin 3.

Contents

Introduction

Two things are surprising about Elizabeth Bowen's Irish short stories (that is, her stories set in Ireland) – first, that there are not more of them, and second, that they came so late. Her earliest childhood was spent entirely in Ireland; and even though from the age of seven she spent more time in England than in Ireland, "home" was always Bowen's Court in County Cork until it was sold, when she was over fifty. Her first volume of stories came out in 1923; yet "Her Table Spread" and "The Tommy Crans", the earliest stories in this collection, came out in 1930 and 1934 respectively, and all the others appeared either during or after the Second World War.

This is not just coincidence. Elizabeth Bowen was in London during that war, in the thick of things. She served as an Air Raid Patrol warden; her husband was an Englishman who had been decorated in the First World War. She identified fiercely with England's struggle and was a great admirer of Churchill. This made her relation to her own "Irishness" more poignant. On her trips to Ireland researching Irish opinion for the British Ministry of Information, she perhaps felt like the Irishman in "Sunday Afternoon" on a wartime visit to friends in neutral Ireland: "He could feel with a shock . . . how insensibly he had deserted, these last years, the aesthetic of living he had got from them."

There was this feeling of alienation; but it was balanced by a growing sense of Ireland as the place of peace and the true home. She wrote the story "The Happy Autumn Fields" in a borrowed flat after she had been bombed out of her London house: the shattering experience is exorcised by the dream of an ordered nineteenth-century country existence, whose subtle emotions were as far removed as possible from the grim crude facts of what was happening. There is in fact nothing in this story to suggest that the "happy autumn fields" are specifically Irish ones, but she wrote in her preface to the collection in which the story appeared that the locale "is, though not stated, to me unshakeably County Cork". After the war she came back to Bowen's Court, thinking to make her life there. But for several reasons — most of them financial — this was not to be. She died in England.

It was her vision of Ireland that sharpened in middle life, perhaps because only then could she see it objectively; or perhaps because only then, after long absences, did it take on that "unfamiliar" quality on which her imagination thrived. (*The Last September,* published in 1929 and her only wholly "Irish" novel, is a most subjective work written out of adolescent experience.) She said that she never thought of herself as a "regional" writer: "Imagination of my kind is most caught, most fired, most worked upon by the unfamiliar." Nor would she want us to see her Irish stories of the 1940s and '50s as marking a new phase in her development as a writer:

> "As I see it, a writer of short stories is at his or her best sometimes, and sometimes not . . . 'Development' may appear in any one writer's successive novels; in successive short stories I hold it to be a myth. The short story is a matter of vision, rather than of feeling. . . . Of vision, one asks only that it should not lose its intensity."

The intensity of vision is there, superbly, in at least four of her Irish stories: "The Happy Autumn Fields", "Summer Night", "A Day in the Dark" and "Her Table Spread". Read these first. For me, "Summer Night" is the best; these four are all cinematic, and all powered by a

strong undertow of sexual feeling that is disallowed, inex-
pressible, distant, or doomed. (The only way to transcribe
passions, she wrote, was in "dispassionate understate-
ment".) Sean O'Faolain in his book *The Short Story* (1948)
took "Her Table Spread" as an example to analyse; he has
worthwhile things to say about its compression and cohe-
sion — "a lovely example", he says, of the merging of
situation and construction. (Frank O'Connor in *his* book
on the short story — *The Lonely Voice*, 1963 — does not discuss Bowen at all: an interesting omission.) O'Faolain
makes the point that Valeria in "Her Table Spread" "in
one form or another ... turns up in all Miss Bowen's
novels" — she is certainly first cousin to the extraordinary
central character of her last completed novel, *Eva Trout*.

It is of course possible to trace many themes and
characters from her stories to her novels, and vice versa.
But there is one big divide; she does not bring the supernatural into her novels — she said it was "unethical" — and
it is frequently a factor in the short stories: most happily, in
this collection, in "The Happy Autumn Fields", and less
happily, in my opinion, in "Hand in Glove". She wrote:
"I do not make use of the supernatural as a get-out; it is in-
separable (whether or not it comes to the surface) from my
sense of life." Thus it is in her short stories that she is most
herself, "at once brilliant and limited", as she
characterised, dangerously, most Irish and Anglo-Irish
writing. The short story can, she wrote, approach
"aesthetic and moral truth" more nearly than the novel;
and technically in control, she writes in these stories in the
shadow of a world elsewhere and — like the characters in
"A Day in the Dark" — "on the margin of a passion which
was impossible".

Irish writers have made the short story peculiarly their
own. Comparisons of Elizabeth Bowen's Irish stories with
those of O'Connor, O'Faolain or Mary Lavin might be in-
structive as an academic exercise in literary or social
history. But it is pointless and diminishing to try to grade
these and other major Irish short-story writers of this cen-

tury in a purely Irish hierarchy: they belong not only to Ireland but to the world, and Elizabeth Bowen is among them.

Victoria Glendinning

Sunday Afternoon

'So here you are!' exclaimed Mrs. Vesey to the newcomer who joined the group on the lawn. She reposed for an instant her light, dry fingers on his. 'Henry has come from London,' she added. Acquiescent smiles from the others round her showed that the fact was already known – she was no more than indicating to Henry the role that he was to play. 'What are your experiences? – Please tell us. But nothing dreadful: we are already feeling a little sad.'

'I am sorry to hear that,' said Henry Russel, with the air of one not anxious to speak of his own affairs. Drawing a cane chair into the circle, he looked from face to face with concern. His look travelled on to the screen of lilac, whose dark purple, pink-silver, and white plumes sprayed out in the brilliance of the afternoon. The late May Sunday blazed, but was not warm: something less than a wind, a breath of coldness, fretted the edge of things. Where the lilac barrier ended, across the sun-polished meadows, the Dublin mountains continued to trace their hazy, today almost colourless line. The coldness had been admitted by none of the seven or eight people who, in degrees of elderly beauty, sat here full in the sun, at this sheltered edge of the lawn: they continued to master the coldness, or to deny it, as though with each it were some secret *malaise*. An air of fastidious, stylised melancholy, an air of being secluded behind glass, characterised for Henry these old friends in whose shadow he had grown up. To their pleasure at having him back among them was added, he felt, a taboo or warning – he was to tell a little, but not much. He could feel with a shock, as he sat down, how insensibly he had deserted, these last years, the aesthetic of living that he had got from them. As things were, he felt over him their suspended charm. The democratic smell of the Dublin bus, on which he had made the outward journey to join them, had evaporated from his person by the time he was half-way up Mrs. Vesey's chestnut avenue. Her house, with its fanlights and tall windows, was a villa in the Italian sense, just near enough to the city to make the country's sweetness particularly acute. Now, the sensations of war-time, that locked his inside being, began as surely to be dispelled — in the influence of this eternalised Sunday after-noon.

'Sad?' he said, 'that is quite wrong.'

'These days, our lives seem unreal,' said Mrs. Vesey — with eyes that penetrated his point of view. 'But, worse than that, this afternoon we discover that we all have friends who have died.'

'Lately?' said Henry, tapping his fingers together.

'Yes, in all cases,' said Ronald Cuffe — with just enough dryness to show how much the subject had been beginning to tire him. 'Come, Henry, we look to you for distraction. To us, these days, you are quite a figure. In fact, from all we have heard of London, it is something that you should be alive. Are things there as shocking as they say — or are they more shocking?' he went on, with distaste.

'Henry's not sure,' said someone, 'he looks pontifical.'

Henry, in fact, was just beginning to twiddle this far-off word 'shocking' round in his mind, when a diversion caused some turning of heads. A young girl stepped out of a window and began to come their way across the lawn. She was Maria, Mrs. Vesey's niece. A rug hung over her bare arm: she spread out the rug and sat down at her aunt's feet. With folded arms, and her fingers on her thin pointed elbows, she immediately fixed her eyes on Henry Russel. 'Good afternoon,' she said to him, in a mocking but somehow intimate tone.

The girl, like some young difficult pet animal, seemed in a way to belong to everyone there. Miss Ria Store, the patroness of the arts, who had restlessly been refolding her fur cape, said: 'And where have *you* been, Maria?'

'Indoors.'

Someone said, 'On this beautiful afternoon?'

'Is it?' said Maria, frowning impatiently at the grass.

'Instinct,' said the retired judge, 'now tells Maria it's time for tea.'

'No, this does,' said Maria, nonchalantly showing her wrist with the watch on it. 'It keeps good time, thank you, Sir Isaac.' She returned her eyes to Henry. 'What have you been saying?'

'You interrupted Henry. He had been just going to speak.'

'*Is* it so frightening?' Maria said.

'The bombing?' said Henry. 'Yes. But as it does not connect with the rest of life, it is difficult, you know, to know what one feels. One's feelings seem to have no language for anything so preposterous. As for thoughts – '

'At that rate,' said Maria, with a touch of contempt, 'your thoughts would not be interesting.'

'Maria,' said somebody, 'that is no way to persuade Henry to talk.'

'About what is important,' announced Maria, 'it seems that no one can tell one anything. There is really nothing, till one knows it oneself.'

'Henry is probably right,' said Ronald Cuffe, 'in considering that this – this outrage is *not* important. There is no place for it in human experience; it apparently cannot make a place of its own. It will have no literature.'

'Literature!' said Maria. 'One can see, Mr. Cuffe, that *you* have always been safe!'

'Maria,' said Mrs. Vesey, 'you're rather pert.'

Sir Isaac said, 'What does Maria expect to know?'

Maria pulled off a blade of grass and bit it. Something calculating and passionate appeared in her; she seemed to be crouched up inside herself. She said to Henry sharply: 'But you'll go back, of course?'

'To London? Yes – this is only my holiday. Anyhow,

one cannot stay long away.'

Immediately he had spoken Henry realised how subtly this offended his old friends. Their position was, he saw, more difficult than his own, and he could not have said a more cruel thing. Mrs. Vesey, with her adept smile that was never entirely heartless, said: 'Then we must hope your time here will be pleasant. Is it so very short?'

'And be careful, Henry,' said Ria Store, 'or you will find Maria stowed away in your baggage. And there would be an embarrassment, at an English port! We can feel her planning to leave us at any time.'

Henry said, rather flatly: 'Why should not Maria travel in the ordinary way?'

'Why should Maria travel at all? There is only one journey now – into danger. We cannot feel that that is necessary for her.'

Sir Isaac added: 'We fear, however, that that is the journey Maria wishes to make.'

Maria, curled on the lawn with the nonchalance of a feline creature, through this kept her eyes cast down. Another cold puff came through the lilac, soundlessly knocking the blooms together. One woman, taken quite unawares, shivered – then changed this into a laugh. There was an aside about love from Miss Store, who spoke with a cold, abstracted knowledge – 'Maria has no experience, none whatever; she hopes to meet heroes – she meets none. So now she hopes to find heroes across the sea. Why, Henry, she might make a hero of you.'

'It is not that,' said Maria, who had heard. Mrs. Vesey bent down and touched her shoulder; she sent the girl into the house to see if tea were ready. Presently they all rose and followed – in twos and threes, heads either erect composedly or else deliberately bowed in thought. Henry knew the idea of summer had been relinquished: they would not return to the lawn again. In the dining-room – where the white walls and the glass of the pictures held the reflections of summers – burned the log fire they were so glad to see. With her shoulder against the mantelpiece stood Maria, watching them take their places at the round table. Everything Henry had heard said had fallen off her – in these few minutes all by herself she had started in again on a fresh phase of living that was intact and pure. So much so, that Henry felt the ruthlessness of her disregard for the past, even the past of a few minutes ago. She came forward and put her hands on two chairs – to show she had been keeping a place for him.

Lady Ottery, leaning across the table, said: 'I must ask you – we heard you had lost everything. But that cannot be true?'

Henry said, unwillingly: 'It's true that I lost my flat, and everything in my flat.'

'*Henry,*' said Mrs. Vesey, 'all your beautiful things?'

'Oh dear,' said Lady Ottery, overpowered, 'I thought that could not be possible. I ought not to have asked.'

Ria Store looked at Henry critically. 'You take this too calmly. What has happened to you?'

'It was some time ago. And it happens to many people.'

'But not to everyone,' said Miss Store. 'I should see no reason, for instance, why it should happen to me.'

'One cannot help looking at you,' said Sir Isaac. 'You must forgive our amazement. But there was a time, Henry, when I think we all used to feel that we knew you well. If this is not a painful question, at this juncture, why did you not send your valuables out of town? You could have even shipped them over to us.'

'I was attached to them. I wanted to live with them.'

'And now,' said Miss Store, 'you live with nothing, for ever. Can you really feel that that is life?'

'I do. I may be easily pleased. It was by chance I was out when the place was hit. You may feel – and I honour your point of view – that I should have preferred, at my age, to go into eternity with some pieces of glass and jade and a dozen pictures. But, in fact, I am very glad to remain. To exist.'

'On what level?'

'On any level.'

'Come, Henry,' said Ronald Cuffe, 'that is a cynicism one cannot like in you. You speak of your age: to us, of course, that is nothing. You are at your maturity.'

'Forty-three.'

Maria gave Henry an askance look, as though, after all, he were not a friend. But she then said: 'Why should he wish he was dead?' Her gesture upset some tea on the lace cloth, and she idly rubbed it up with her handkerchief. The tug her rubbing gave to the cloth shook a petal from a Chinese peony in the centre bowl on to a plate of cucumber sandwiches. This little bit of destruction was watched by the older people in fascination, with a kind of appeasement, as though it were a guarantee against something worse.

'Henry is not young and savage, like you are. Henry's life is – or was – an affair of attachments,' said Ria Store. She turned her eyes, under their lids, on Henry. 'I wonder how much of you *has* been blown to blazes.'

'I have no way of knowing,' he said. 'Perhaps you have?'

'Chocolate cake?' said Maria.

'Please.'

For chocolate layer cake, the Vesey cook had been famous since Henry was a boy of seven or eight. The look, then the taste, of the brown segment linked him with Sunday afternoons when he had been brought here by his mother; then, with a phase of his adolescence when he had been unable to eat, only able to look round. Mrs. Vesey's beauty, at that time approaching its last lunar quarter, had swum on him when he was about nineteen. In Maria, child of her brother's late marriage, he now saw that beauty, or sort of physical genius, at the start. In Maria, this without hesitation, without the halting influence that had bound Mrs. Vesey up – yes, and bound Henry up, from his boyhood, with her – in a circle of quizzical half-smiles. In revenge, he accused the young girl who moved him – who seemed framed, by some sort of anticipation, for the new catastrophic *outward* order of life – of brutality, of being

14

without spirit. At his age, between two generations, he felt cast out. He felt Mrs. Vesey might not forgive him for having left her for a world at war.

Mrs. Vesey blew out the blue flame under the kettle, and let the silver trapdoor down with a snap. She then gave exactly one of those smiles – at the same time, it was the smile of his mother's friend. Ronald Cuffe picked the petal from the sandwiches and rolled it between his fingers, waiting for her to speak.

'It is cold, *indoors,*' said Mrs. Vesey. 'Maria, put another log on the fire. – Ria, you say the most unfortunate things. We must remember Henry has had a shock. – Henry, let us talk about something better. You work in an office, then, since the war?'

'In a Ministry – in an office, yes.'

'Very hard? – Maria, that is all you would do if you went to England: work in an office. This is not like a war in history, you know.'

Maria said: 'It is not in history yet.' She licked round her lips for the rest of the chocolate taste, then pushed her chair a little back from the table. She looked secretively at her wrist-watch. Henry wondered what the importance of time could be.

He learned what the importance of time was when, on his way down the avenue to the bus, he found Maria between two chestnut trees. She slanted up to him and put her hand on the inside of his elbow. Faded dark-pink stamen from the flowers above them had moulted down on to her hair. 'You have ten minutes more, really,' she said. 'They sent you off ten minutes before your time. They are frightened someone would miss the bus and come back; then everything would have to begin again. As it is always the same, you would not think it would be so difficult for my aunt.'

'Don't talk like that; it's unfeeling; I don't like it,' said Henry, stiffening his elbow inside Maria's grasp.

'Very well, then: walk to the gate, then back. I shall be able to hear your bus coming. It's true what they said – I'm

15

intending to go away. They will have to make up something without me.'

'Maria, I can't like you. Everything you say is destructive and horrible.'

'Destructive? – I thought you didn't mind.'

'I still want the past.'

'Then how weak you are,' said Maria. 'At tea I admired you. The past – things done over and over again with more trouble than they were ever worth? – However, there's no time to talk about that. Listen, Henry: I must have your address. I suppose you *have* an address now?' She stopped him, just inside the white gate with the green drippings: here he blew stamen off a page of his notebook, wrote on the page and tore it out for her. 'Thank you,' said Maria, 'I might turn up – if I wanted money, or anything. But there will be plenty to do: I can drive a car.'

Henry said: 'I want you to understand that I won't be party to this – *in any way.*'

She shrugged and said: 'You want *them* to understand' – and sent a look back to the house. Whereupon, on his entire being, the suspend＜ charm of the afternoon worked. He protested against the return to the zone of death, and perhaps never ever seeing all this again. The cruciform lilac flowers, in all their purples, and the colourless mountains behind Mrs. Vesey's face besought him. The moment he had been dreading, returning desire, flooded him in this tunnel of avenue, with motors swishing along the road outside and Maria standing staring at him. He adored the stoicism of the group he had quitted – with their little fears and their great doubts – the grace of the thing done over again. He thought, with nothing left but our brute courage, we shall be nothing but brutes.

'What is the matter?' Maria said. Henry did not answer: they turned and walked to and fro inside the gates. Shadow played over her dress and hair: feeling the disenchantedness of his look at her she asked again, uneasily, 'What's the matter?'

'You know,' he said, 'when you come away from here,

16

no one will care any more that you are Maria. You will no longer be Maria, as a matter of fact. Those looks, those things that are said to you – they make you, you silly little girl. You are you only inside their spell. You may think action is better – but who will care for you when you only act? You will have an identity number, but no identity. Your whole existence has been in contradistinction. You may think you want an ordinary fate – but there is no ordinary fate. And that extraordinariness in the fate of each of us is only recognised by your aunt. I admit that her view of life is too much for me – that is why I was so stiff and touchy today. But where shall we be when nobody has a view of life?'

'You don't expect me to understand you, do you?'

'Even your being a savage, even being scornful – Yes, even that you have got from them. – Is that my bus?'

'At the other side of the river: it has still got to cross the bridge. – Henry – ' she put face up. He touched it with kisses thoughtful and cold. 'Good-bye,' he said, 'Miranda.'

' – Maria – '

'Miranda. This is the end of *you*. Perhaps it is just as well.'

'I'll be seeing you – '

'You'll come round my door in London – with your little new number chained to your wrist.'

'The trouble with you is, you're half old.'

Maria ran out through the gates to stop the bus, and Henry got on to it and was quickly carried away.

Her Table Spread

Alban had few opinions on the subject of marriage; his attitude to women was negative, but in particular he was not attracted to Miss Cuffe. Coming down early for dinner, red satin dress cut low, she attacked the silence with loud laughter before he had spoken. He recollected having heard that she was abnormal — at twenty-five, of statuesque development, still detained in childhood. The two other ladies, in beaded satins, made entrances of a surprising formality. It occurred to him, his presence must constitute an occasion: they certainly sparkled. Old Mr Rossiter, uncle to Mrs. Treye, came last, more sourly. They sat for some time without the addition of lamplight. Dinner was not announced; the ladies, by remaining on guard, seemed to deprecate any question of its appearance. No sound came from other parts of the Castle.

Miss Cuffe was an heiress to whom the Castle belonged and whose guests they all were. But she carefully followed the movements of her aunt, Mrs. Treye; her ox-eyes moved from face to face in happy submission rather than expectancy. She was continually preoccupied with attempts at gravity, as though holding down her skirts in a high wind. Mrs. Treye and Miss Carbin combined to cover her excitement; still, their looks frequently stole from the company to the windows, of which there were too many. He received a strong impression someone outside was waiting to come in. At last, with a sigh they got up: dinner had been announced.

The Castle was built on high ground, commanding the estuary; a steep hill, with trees, continued above it. On fine days the view was remarkable, of almost Italian brilliance, with that constant reflection up from the water that even now prolonged the too-long day. Now, in continuous evening rain, the winding wooded line of the further shore could be seen and, nearer the windows, a smothered island with the stump of a watch-tower. Where the Castle stood, a higher tower had answered the island's. Later a keep, then wings, had been added: now the fine peaceful residence had French windows opening on to the terrace. Invasions from the water would henceforth be social, perhaps amorous. On the slope down from the terrace, trees began again; almost, but not quite concealing the destroyer. Alban, who knew nothing, had not yet looked down.

It was Mr Rossiter who first spoke of the destroyer – Alban meanwhile glancing along the table; the preparations had been stupendous. The destroyer had come today. The ladies all turned to Alban: the beads on their bosoms sparkled. So this was what they had here, under their trees. Engulfed by their pleasure, from now on he disappeared personally. Mr. Rossiter, rising a note, continued. The estuary, it appeared, was deep, with a channel buoyed up it. By a term of the Treaty, English ships were permitted to anchor in these waters.

'But the've been afraid of the rain!' chimed in Valeria Cuffe.

'Hush,' said her aunt, 'that's silly. Sailors would be acccustomed to getting wet.'

But, Miss Carbin reported, that spring there *had* already been one destroyer. Two of the officers had been seen dancing at the hotel at the head of the estuary.

'So' said Alban, 'you are quite in the world.' He adjusted his glasses in her direction.

Miss Carbin – blonde, not forty, and an attachment of Mrs. Treye's – shook her head despondently. 'We were all away at Easter. Wasn't it curious they should have come then? The sailors walked in the demesne but never touched the daffodils.'

'As though I should have cared!' exclaimed Valeria passionately.

'Morale too good,' stated Mr. Rossiter.

'But next evening,' continued Miss Carbin, 'the officers did not go to the hotel. They climbed up here through the trees to the terrace — you see, they had no idea. Friends of ours were staying here at the Castle, and they apologised. Our friends invited them in to supper . . .'

'Did they accept?'

The three ladies said in a breath: 'Yes, they came.'

Valeria added urgently, 'So don't you *think* — ?'

'So tonight we have a destroyer to greet you,' Mrs. Treye said quickly to Alban. 'It is quite an event; the country people are coming down from the mountains. These waters are very lonely; the steamers have given up since the bad times; there is hardly a pleasure boat. The weather this year has driven visitors right away.'

'You are beautifully remote.'

'Yes,' agreed Miss Carbin. 'Do you know much about the Navy? Do you think, for instance, that this is likely to be the same destroyer?'

'Will they remember?' Valeria's bust was almost on the table. But with a rustle Mrs. Treye pressed Valeria's toe. For the diningroom also looked out across the estuary, and the great girl had not once taken her eyes from the window. Perhaps it was unfotunate that Mr. Alban should have coincided with the destroyer. Perhaps it was unfortunate for Mr. Alban too.

For he saw now he was less than half the feast; unappeased, the party sat looking through him, all grouped at the end of the table — to the other, chairs had been pulled up. Dinner was being served very slowly. Candles — possible to see from the water — were lit now; some wet peonies glistened. Outside, day still lingered hopefully. The bushes over the edge of the terrace were like heads — you could have sworn sometimes you saw them mounting, swaying in manly talk. Once, wound up in the rain, a bird whistled, seeming hardly a bird.

'Perhaps since then they have been to Greece, or Malta?'

'That would be the Mediterranean fleet,' said Mr. Rossiter.

They were sorry to think of anything out in the rain tonight.

'The decks must be streaming,' said Miss Carbin.

Then Valeria, exclaiming, 'Please excuse me!' pushed her chain in and ran from the room.

'She is impulsive' explained Mrs. Treye. 'Have *you* been to Malta, Mr. Alban?'

In the drawing-room, empty of Valeria, the standard lamps had been lit. Through their ballet-skirt shades, rose and lemon, they gave out a deep, welcoming light. Alban, at the ladies' invitation, undraped the piano. He played, but they could see he was not pleased. It was obvious he had always been a civilian and when he had taken his place on the piano stool – which he twirled round three times, rather fussily – his dinner-jacket wrinkled across the shoulders. It was sad they should feel so indifferent, for he came from London. Mendelssohn was exasperating to them – they opened all four windows to let the music downhill. They preferred not to draw the curtains; the air, though damp, being pleasant tonight, they said.

The piano was damp, but Alban played almost all his heart out. He played out the indignation of years his mild manner concealed. He had failed to love; nobody did anything about this; partners at dinner gave him less than half their attention. He knew some spring had dried up at the root of the world. He was fixed in the dark rain, by an indifferent shore. He played badly, but they were unmusical. Old Mr. Rossiter, who was not what he seemed, went back to the dining-room to talk to the parlourmaid.

Valeria, glittering vastly, appeared in a window.

'Come *in*!' her aunt cried in indignation. She would die of a chill, childless, in fact unwedded; the Castle would have to be sold and where would they all be?

But – 'Lights down there!' Valeria shouted above the music.

They had to run out for a moment, laughing and holding cushions over their bare shoulders. Alban left the piano; they looked boldly down from the terrace. Indeed, there they were: two lights like arc-lamps, blurred by rain and drawn down deep in reflection into the steady water. There were, too, ever so many portholes, all lit up.

'Perhaps they are playing bridge,' said Miss Carbin.

'Now I wonder if Uncle Robert ought to have called,' said Mrs. Treye. 'Perhaps we have seemed remiss – one calls on a regiment.'

'Patrick could row him out tomorrow.'

'He hates the water.' She sighed. 'Perhaps they will be gone.'

'Let's go for a row now – let's go for a row with a lantern,' besought Valeria, jumping and pulling her aunt's elbow. They produced such indignation she disappeared again – wet satin skirts and all – into the bushes. The ladies could do no more: Alban suggested the rain might spot their dresses.

'They must lose a great deal, playing cards throughout an evening for high stakes,' Miss Carbin said with concern as they all sat down again.

'Yet, if you come to think of it, somebody must win.'

But the naval officers who so joyfully supped at Easter had been, Miss Carbin knew, a Mr. Graves, and a Mr. Garrett: *they* would certainly lose. 'At all events, it is better than dancing at the hotel; there would be nobody of their type.'

'There is nobody there at all.'

'I expect they are best where they are . . . Mr. Alban, a Viennese waltz?'

He played while the ladies whispered, waving the waltz time a little distractedly. Mr. Rossiter, coming back, momentously stood: they turned in hope: even the waltz halted. But he brought no news. 'You should call Valeria in. You can't tell who may be round the place. She's not fit to be out tonight.'

'Perhaps she's not out.'

'She is,' said Mr. Rossiter crossly. 'I just saw her racing past the window with a lantern.'

Valeria's mind was made up: she was a princess. Not for nothing had she had the dining-room silver polished and all set out. She would pace around in red satin that swished behind, while Mr. Alban kept on playing a loud waltz. They would be dazed at all she had to offer – also her two new statues and the leopard skin from the auction.

When he and she were married (she inclined a little to Mr. Garrett) they would invite all the Navy up the estuary and give them tea. Her estuary would be filled up, like a regatta, with loud excited battleships tooting to one another and flags flying. The terrace would be covered with grateful sailors, leaving room for the band. She would keep the peacocks her aunt did not allow. His friends would be surprised to notice that Mr. Garrett had meanwhile become an admiral, all gold. He would lead the other admirals into the Castle and say, while they wiped their feet respectfully: 'These are my wife's statues; she has given them to me. One is Mars, one is Mercury. We have a Venus, but she is not dressed. And wait till I show you our silver and gold plates . . .' The Navy would be unable to tear itself away.

She had been excited for some weeks at the idea of marrying Mr. Alban, but now the lovely appearance of the destroyer put him out of her mind. He would not have done; he was not handsome. But she could keep him to play the piano on quiet afternoons.

Her friends had told her Mr. Garrett was quite a Viking. She was so very familiar with his appearance that she felt sometimes they had already been married for years – though still, sometimes, he could not realise his good luck. She still had to remind him the island was hers too . . . Tonight, Aunt and darling Miss Carbin had so fallen in with her plans, putting on their satins and decorating the drawing-room, that the dinner became a betrothal feast. There was some little hitch about the arrival of Mr. Garrett – she had heard that gentlemen sometimes could not tie

23

their ties. And now he was late and would be discouraged. So she must now go half way down to the water and wave a lantern.

But she put her two hands over the lantern, then smothered it in her dress. She had a panic. Supposing she should prefer Mr. Graves?

She had heard Mr. Graves was stocky, but very merry; when he came to supper at Easter he slid in the gallery. He would teach her to dance, and take her to Naples and Paris ... Oh dear, oh dear, then they must fight for her; that was all there was to it ... She let the lantern out of her skirts and waved. Her fine arm with bangles went up and down, up and down, with the staggering light, the trees one by one jumped up from the dark, like savages.

Inconceivably, the destroyer took no notice.

Undisturbed by oars, the rain stood up from the water; not a light rose to peer, and the gramophone, though it remained very faint did not cease or alter.

In mackintoshes, Mr. Rossiter and Alban meanwhile made their way to the boathouse, Alban did not know why. 'If that goes on,' said Mr. Rossiter, nodding towards Valeria's lantern, 'they'll fire one of their guns at us.'

'Oh, no. Why?' said Alban. He buttoned up, however, the collar of his mackintosh.

'Nervous as cats. It's high time that girl was married. She's a nice girl in many ways, too.'

'Couldn't we get the lantern away from her?' They stepped on a paved causeway and heard the water nibble the rocks.

'She'd scream the place down. She's of age now, you see.'

'But if —'

'Oh, she won't do that; I was having a bit of fun with you.' Chuckling equably, Mrs. Treye's uncle unlocked and pulled open the boathouse door. A bat whistled out.

'Why are we here?'

'She might come for the boat; she's a fine oar,' said Mr. Rossiter wisely. The place was familiar to him; he lit an oil

24

lamp and, sitting down on a trestle with a staunch air of having done what he could, reached a bottle of whisky out of the boat. He motioned the bottle to Alban. 'It's a wild night,' he said. 'Ah, well, we don't have these destroyers every day.'

'That seems fortunate.'

'Well, it is and it isn't.' Restoring the bottle to the vertical, Mr. Rossiter continued: 'It's a pity you don't want a wife. You'd be the better for a wife, d'you see, a young fellow like you. She's got a nice character; she's a girl you could shape. She's got a nice income.' The bat returned from the rain and knocked round the lamp. Lowering the bottle frequently, Mr. Rossiter talked to Alban (whose attitude remained negative) of women in general and the parlourmaid in particular . . .

'*Bat!*' Alban squealed irrepressibly, and with his hand to his ear — where he still felt it — fled from the boathouse. Mr. Rossiter's conversation continued. Alban's pumps squelched as he ran; he skidded along the causeway and baulked at the upward steps. His soul squelched equally: he had been warned, he had been warned. He had heard they were all mad; he had erred out of headiness and curiosity. A degree of terror was agreeable to his vanity: by express wish he had occupied haunted rooms. Now he had no other pumps in this country, no idea where to buy them, and a ducal visit ahead. Also, wandering as it were among the apples and amphoras of an art school, he had blundered into the life room: woman revolved gravely.

'Hell,' he said to the steps, mounting, his mind blank to the outcome.

He was nerved for the jumping lantern, but half way up to the Castle darkness was once more absolute. Her lantern had gone out; he could orientate himself — in spite of himself — by her sobbing. Absolute desperation. He pulled up so short that, for balance, he had to cling to a creaking tree.

'Hi!' she croaked. Then: 'You *are* there! I hear you!'

'Miss Cuffe —'

25

'How too bad you are! I never heard you rowing. I thought you were never coming –'

'Quietly, my dear girl.'

'Come up quickly. I haven't even seen you. Come up to the windows –'

'Miss Cuffe –'

'Don't you remember the way?' As sure but not so noiseless as a cat in the dark, Valeria hurried to him.

'Mr. Garrett –' she panted. 'I'm Miss Cuffe. Where have you been? I've destroyed my beautiful red dress and they've eaten up your dinner. But we're still waiting. Don't be afraid; you'll soon be there now. I'm Miss Cuffe; this is my Castle –'

'Listen, it's I, Mr. Alban –'

'Ssh, ssh, Mr. Alban: *Mr. Garrett has landed.*'

Her cry, his voice, some breath of the joyful intelligence brought the others on to the terrace, blind with lamplight.

'Valeria?'

'Mr. Garrett has landed!'

Mrs. Treye said to Miss Carbin under her breath, 'Mr. Garrett has come.'

Miss Carbin, half weeping with agitation, replied, 'We must go in.' But uncertain who was to speak next, or how to speak, they remained leaning over the darkness. Behind, through the windows, lamps spread great skirts of light. The dumb keyboard shone like a ballroom floor.

Alban, looking up, saw their arms and shoulders under the bright rain. Close by, Valeria's fingers creaked on her warm wet satin. She laughed like a princess, magnificently justified. Their unseen faces were all three lovely, and, in the silence after the laughter, such a strong tenderness reached him that, standing there in full manhood, he was for a moment not exiled. For the moment, without moving or speaking, he stood, in the dark, in a flame, as though all three said: 'My darling . . .'

Perhaps it was best for them all that early, when next day first lightened the rain, the destroyer steamed out – below the extinguished Castle where Valeria lay with her arms wide, past the boathouse where Mr. Rossiter lay insensible and the bat hung masked in its wings — down the estuary into the open sea.

The Tommy Crans

Herbert's feet, from dangling so long in the tram, had died of cold in his boots; he stamped the couple of coffins on blue-and-buff mosaic. In the Tommy Crans' cloak-room the pegs were too high – Uncle Archer cocked H.M.S. *Terrible* for him over a checked ulster. Tommy Cran – aslant meanwhile, in the doorway – was an enormous presence. 'Come on, now, come!' he exclaimed, and roared with impatience. You would have said he was also arriving at the Tommy Crans' Christmas party, of which one could not bear to miss a moment.

Now into the hall Mrs. Tommy Cran came swimming from elsewhere, dividing with curved little strokes the festive air – hyacinths and gunpowder. Her sleeves, in a thousand ruffles, fled from her elbows. She gained Uncle Archer's lapels and, bobbing, floated from this attachment. Uncle Archer, verifying the mistletoe, loudly kissed her face of delicate pink sugar. 'Ha!' yelled Tommy, drawing an unseen dagger. Herbert laughed with embarrassment.

'Only think, Nancy let off all the crackers before tea! She's quite wild, but there are more behind the piano. Ah, is this little Herbert? Herbert . . .'

'Very well, thank you,' said Herbert, and shook hands defensively. This was his first Christmas Day without any father; the news went before him. He had seen his mother off, very brave with the holly wreath, in the cemetery tram. She and father were spending Christmas afternoon together.

Mrs. Tommy Cran stooped to him, bright with a tear-glitter, then with a strong upward sweep, like an angel's, bore him to gaiety. 'Fancy Nancy!' He fancied Nancy. So by now they would all be wearing the paper caps. Flinging back a white door, she raced Herbert elsewhere.

The room where they all sat seemed to be made of glass, it collected the whole daylight; the candles were still waiting. Over the garden, day still hung like a pink flag; over the trees like frozen feathers, the enchanted icy lake, the lawn. The table was in the window. As Herbert was brought in a clock struck four; the laughing heads all turned in a silence brief as a breath's intake. The great many gentlemen and the rejoicing ladies leaned apart; he and Nancy looked at each other gravely.

He saw Nancy, crowned and serious because she was a queen. Advanced by some urgent pushing, he made his way round the table and sat down beside her, podgily.

She said: 'How d'you do? Did you see our lake? It is all frozen. Did you ever see our lake before?'

'I never came here.'

'Did you see our two swans?'

She was so beautiful, rolling her ringlets, round with light, on her lacy shoulders, that he said rather shortly: 'I shouldn't have thought your lake was large enough for two swans.'

'It is, indeed,' said Nancy; 'it goes round the island. It's large enough for a boat.'

They were waiting, around the Christmas cake, for tea to be brought in. Mrs. Tommy Cran shook out the ribbons of her guitar and began to sing again. Very quietly, for a secret, he and Nancy crept to the window; she showed how the lake wound; he could guess how, in summer, her boat would go pushing among the lily leaves. She showed him their boat-house, rusty-red from a lamp inside, solid. 'We had a lamp put there for the poor cold swans.' (And the swans were asleep beside it.) 'How old are you, Herbert?'

'Eight.'

'Oh, I'm nine. Do you play brigands?'

'I could,' said Herbert.

'Oh, I don't; I'd hate to. But I know some boys who do. Did you have many presents? Uncle Ponto brought me a train; it's more suitable for a boy, really. I could give it to you, perhaps.'

'How many uncles —— ?' began Herbert.

'Ten pretence and none really. I'm adopted, because mummy and daddy have no children. I think that's better fun, don't you?

'Yes,' replied Herbert, after consideration; 'anybody could be born.'

All the time, Nancy had not ceased to look at him seriously and impersonally. They were both tired already by this afternoon of boisterous grown-up society; they would have liked to be quiet, and though she was loved by ten .magic uncles and wore a pearl locket, and he was fat, with spectacles, and felt deformed a little from everybody's knowing about his father, they felt at ease in each other's company.

'Nancy, cut the cake!' exclaimed Mrs. Tommy, and they all clapped their hands for Nancy's attention. So the coloured candles were lit, the garden went dark with loneliness and was immediately curtained out. Two of the uncles put rugs on and bounded about the room like bears and lions; the other faces drew out a crimson brand round the silver teapot. Mrs. Tommy could not bear to put down the guitar, so the teapot fell into the hands of a fuzzy lady with several husbands who cried 'Ah, don't, now!' and had to keep brushing gentlemen's hands from her waist. And all the others leaned on each other's shoulders and laughed with gladness because they had been asked to the Tommy Crans'; a dozen times everyone died of laughter and rose again, redder ghosts. Teacups whizzed down a chain of hands. Now Nancy, standing up very straight to cut the cake, was like a doll stitched upright into its box, apt, if you should cut the string at the back, to pitch right forward and break its delicate fingers.

'Oh dear,' she sighed, as the knife skidded over the ic-ing. But nobody heard but Herbert. For someone, seeing her white frock over that palace of cake, proposed 'The health of the bride'. And an Uncle Joseph, tipping the tea about in his cup, stared and stared with juicy eyes. But nobody saw but Herbert.

'After tea,' she whispered, 'we'll go and stand on the lake.' And after tea they did, while the others played hide and seek. Herbert, once looking back through a window, saw uncles chasing the laughing aunts. It was not cold on the lake. Nancy said: 'I never believed in fairies — did you either?' She told him she had been given a white muff and was going to be an organist, with an organ of her own. She was going up to Belfast next month to dance for charity. She said she would not give him the train after all; she would give him something really her own, a pink glass greyhound that was an ornament.

When Uncle Archer and Herbert left to walk to the tram terminus, the party was at its brightest. They were singing 'Hark the herald' around the drawing-room piano: Nancy sat on her Uncle Joseph's knee, more than politely.

Uncle Archer did not want to go home either. 'That was a nice little girl,' he said. 'Eh?'

Herbert nodded. His uncle, glad that the little chap hadn't had, after all, such a dismal Christmas, pursued heartily: 'Kiss her?' Herbert looked quite blank. To tell the truth, this had never occurred to him.

He kissed Nancy later; his death, even, was indirectly caused by his loss of her; but their interchanges were never passionate, and he never knew her better than when they had been standing out on the lake, beyond the cheerful windows. Herbert's mother did not know Uncle Archer's merry friends: she had always loved to live quietly, and, as her need for comfort decreased, she and Herbert saw less, or at least as little as ever of Uncle Archer. So that for years Herbert was not taken again across Dublin to the house with the lake. Once he saw Nancy carry her white muff into a shop, but he stood rooted and did not run after her. Once he saw Mrs. Tommy Cran out in Stephen's Green throwing lollipops to the ducks: but he did not approach; there was nothing to say. He was sent to school, where he painfully learnt to be natural with boys: his sight got no better; they said he must wear glasses all his life. Years later, however, when Herbert was thirteen, the Crans gave a dancing-party and did not forget him. He danced once with Nancy; she was silenter now, but she said: 'Why did you never come back again?' He could not explain; he trod on her toes and danced heavily on. A Chinese lantern blazed up, and in the confusion he lost her. That evening he saw Mrs. Tommy in tears in the conservatory. Nancy clung, pressing her head, with its drooping pink ribbons, to Mrs. Cran's shoulder; pressing, perhaps, the shoulder against the head. Soon it was all right again and Mrs. Tommy led off in 'Sir Roger', but Nancy was like a ghost who presently vanished. A week afterwards he had a letter:

Please meet me to tea at Mitchell's; I want your advice specially.

She was distracted: she had come in to Dublin to sell her gold wrist-watch. The Tommy Crans had lost all their money — it wasn't fair to expect them to keep it; they were generous and gay. Nancy had to think hard what must they all do. Herbert went round with her from jeweller to jeweller: these all laughed and paid her nothing but compliments. Her face, with those delicate lovely eyebrows, grew tragic under the fur cap; it rained continuously; she and Herbert looked with incredulity into the grown-up faces: they wondered how one could penetrate far into life without despair. At last a man on the quays gave her eight-and-six for the watch. Herbert, meanwhile, had spent eight shillings of his pocket-money on their cab — and, even so, her darling feet were sodden. They were surprised to see, from the window, Tommy Cran jump from an outside car and run joyfully into the Shelbourne. It turned out he had raised some more money from somewhere — as he deserved.

So he sold the house with the lake and moved to an ornamental castle by Dublin Bay. In spite of the grey scene, the transitory light from the sea, the terrace here was gay with urns of geraniums, magnificent with a descent of steps – scrolls and whorls of balustrade, all the grandeur of stucco. Here the band played for their afternoon parties, and here, when they were twenty and twenty-one, Herbert asked Nancy to marry him.

A pug harnessed with bells ran jingling about the terrace. 'Oh, I don't know, Herbert; I don't know.'

'Do you think you don't love me?'

'I don't know whom I love. Everything would have to be different. Herbert, I don't see how we are ever to live; we seem to know everything. Surely there should be something for us we don't know?' She shut her eyes; they kissed seriously and searchingly. In his arms her body felt soft and voluminous; he could not touch her because of a great fur coat. The coat had been a surprise from Tommy Cran, who loved to give presents on delightful occasions – for now they were off to the Riviera. They were sailing in four days; Nancy and Mrs. Tommy had still all their shopping to do, all his money to spend – he loved them both to be elegant. There was that last party to give before leaving home. Mrs. Tommy could hardly leave the telephone; crossing London, they were to give yet another party, at the Euston Hotel.

'And how could I leave them?' she asked. 'They're my business.'

'Because they are not quite your parents?'

'Oh, no,' she said, eyes reproachful for the misunderstanding he had put up, she knew, only from bitterness. 'They would be my affair whoever I was. Don't you see, they're like that.'

The Tommy Crans returned from the Riviera subdued, and gave no more parties than they could avoid. They hung sun-yellow curtains, in imitation of the Midi, in all the castle windows, and fortified themselves against despair. They warned their friends they were ruined; they

33

honestly were — and there were heartfelt evenings of consolation. After such evenings Mrs. Tommy, awaking heavily, whimpered in Nancy's arms, and Tommy approached silence. They had the highest opinion of Nancy, and were restored by her confidence. She knew they would be all right; she assured them they were the best, the happiest people; they were popular — look how Life came back again and again to beg their pardon. And, just to show them, she accepted Jeremy Neath and his thousands. So the world could see she was lucky; the world saw the Tommy Crans and their daughter had all the luck. To Herbert she explained nothing. She expected everything of him, on behalf of the Tommy Crans.

The two Crans were distracted by her apotheosis from the incident of their ruin. They had seen her queen of a perpetual Christmas party for six months before they themselves came down magnificently, like an empire. Then Nancy came to fetch them over to England, where her husband had found a small appointment for Tommy, excuse for a pension. But Tommy would not want that long; he had a scheme already, a stunner, a certainty; you just wrote to a hundred people and put in half a crown. That last night he ran about with the leaflets, up and down the uncarpeted castle stairs that were his no longer. He offered to let Herbert in on it; he would yet see Herbert a rich man.

Herbert and Nancy walked after dark on the terrace: she looked ill, tired; she was going to have a baby.

'When I asked you to marry me,' he said, 'you never answered. You've never answered yet.'

She said: 'There was no answer. We could never have loved each other and we shall always love each other. We are related.'

Herbert, a heavy un-young young man, walked, past desperation, beside her. He did not want peace, but a sword. He returned again and again to the unique moment of her strangeness to him before, as a child, she had spoken. Before, bewildered by all the laughter, he had realised she also was silent.

'You never played games,' he said, 'or believed in fairies, or anything. I'd have played any game your way; I'd have been good at them. You let them pull all the crackers before tea: now I'd have loved those crackers. That day we met at Mitchell's to sell your watch, you wouldn't have sugar cakes, though I wanted to comfort you. You never asked me out to go round the island in your boat; I'd have died to do that. I never even saw your swans awake. You hold back everything from me and expect me to understand. Why should I understand? In the name of God, what game are we playing?'

'But you do understand?'

'Oh, God,' he cried in revulsion. 'I don't want to! And now you're going to have a stranger child.'

Her sad voice in the dark said: 'You said then, "Anybody could be born!" Herbert, you and I have nothing to do with children — this must be a child like them.'

As they turned back to face the window, her smile and voice were tender, but not for him. In the brightly lit stripped room the Tommy Crans walked about together, like lovers in their freedom from one another. They talked of the fortune to be made, the child to be born. Tommy flung his chest out and moved his arms freely in air he did not possess; here and there, pink leaflets fluttered into the dark. The Tommy Crans would go on for ever and be continued; their seed should never fail.

A Love Story

Mist lay over the estuary, over the terrace, over the hollows of the gummy, sub-tropical garden of the hotel. Now and then a soft, sucking sigh came from the water, as though someone were turning over in his sleep. At the head of the steps down to the boathouse, a patch of hydrangeas still flowered and rotted, though it was December. It was now six o'clock, dark — chinks of light from the hotel lay yellow and blurred on the density. The mist's muffling silence could be everywhere felt. Light from the double glass doors fell down the damp steps. At the head of the steps the cast-iron standard lamps were unlit.

Inside the double glass doors, the lounge with its high curtained bow windows was empty. Brilliantly hotly lit by electric light, it looked like a stage on which there has been a hitch. Light blared on the *vieux rose* curtains and on the ocean of carpet with its jazz design. The armchairs and settees with their taut stuffing had an air of brutal, resilient strength. Brass ashtrays without a segment of ash stood on small tables dotted over the lounge. A glass screen kept the lounge from any draughts from the door; a glass screen protected the lounge from the stairs. But there was nothing to dread: the heating was on, only a smell of tinder-dry turkey carpet, ivory paint, polish and radiators came downstairs from the empty floors above. In the immense tiled fireplace a fire burned with a visible, silent roar.

From a cabinet came a voice announcing the six o'clock war news. In the middle of this, three berries fell from a vase of holly and pattered noisily into a brass tray. The temperate voice of the announcer paused for a moment, halfway through a disaster, as though disturbed by the noise. A spurt of gas from a coal sent a whicker up through the fire. The unheard news came to an end.

Two women came up the steps and pushed in at the glass doors. Their hair was sticky from the damp of the mist. The girl steered her mother round the screen to the fire, then went across and turned off the wireless. The mother unbuttoned her leather coat and threw it back from her handsome, full chest. Keyed up by the sudden electric light, her manner was swaggering and excitable. She looked with contempt at the wireless cabinet and said: 'I don't care what I hear – now!'

'Do shut up, Mother. Do sit down.'

'Do stop being so nervous of me, Teresa. Whatever do you think I'm going to do?'

Teresa took off her trenchcoat and slung it over a chair, then crossed the lounge with her loose, cross walk, in her slacks. 'I know what you want,' she said flatly, ringing the bell. She sat down in an armchair by the fire and stuck her young slender jaw out and crossed her legs. Her mother stayed standing up, with her shoulders braced back; she kept pushing her hair back from her forehead with her long, plump, fine-wristed ringed hand. 'I daresay you're right to be so nervous,' she said. 'I don't know myself what I'll do, from minute to minute. Why did I have to come here – can you tell me that? Why was this the only thing I could do? Do you know when I was last here – who I was with?'

'I suppose I know,' said Teresa, defensively. 'You know you don't want me to understand you, Mother, so I'm not trying to.'

'It's a terrible thing to say,' said Mrs. Massey, 'but it would be better if this had happened to you. I'd rather see you suffer than have no feelings. You're not like a woman, Teresa. And he was your age, not my age.'

'Is that so?' Teresa said, in a voice too lifeless for irony.

Mrs. Massey looked angrily round the lounge and said:

'They've changed the chairs round, since.' She pointed to an empty space on the carpet and said: '*That* was where he sat. ... There isn't even his chair.'

Teresa looked pointedly off down the corridor. 'Michael's coming,' she said. A boy in a white cotton coat, with a dark vivid, Kerry face, beamed at them through the glass screen, then came round the screen for orders. 'Good evening, Michael,' said Teresa.

'Good evening, miss. Good evening to you, ma'am.'

'It's not a good evening for me, I'm afraid, Michael.' Michael lowered his eyes. 'I'm sorry to hear that,' he said, in a trembling and feeling voice. 'It's a long time since we saw you.'

'Does it seem so – ?' Mrs. Massey began wildly. But Teresa put up her hand and in a curt, raised voice ordered her mother's drink. ... 'But I wanted a double,' objected Mrs. Massey, when Michael had gone.

'You know you had that at home,' said Teresa, 'and more than once.' More coldly, she added: 'And how fed up Teddy used to get.'

Frank and Linda, their fingers loosely linked, came downstairs on their way to their private sitting-room. They glanced vacantly through the screen and turned left down the corridor. 'We missed the news again,' she said, as he shut the door. 'We always seem to run late.' 'We can't help that, darling,' he said. Their fire had been made up while they were upstairs. She gave it an unnecessary kick with her heel, and said: 'Did you see those two making a scene in the lounge...'

'I sort of did see the girl,' Frank said. 'Which was the other?'

'I thought they looked like locals in for a drink. Or I daresay they came round here to make a scene. I do think the Irish are exhibitionists.'

'Well, we can't help that, darling, can we?' said Frank, ringing the bell. He sat down in a chair and said: 'Oh, my God ...' Linda dropping into the chair opposite. 'Well, really . . .' Frank said. 'However. I feel fine. I don't care what time it is.'

*   *   *   *

Up in a sitting-room on the first floor. the Perry-Duntons' two dogs slept in front of the fire. bellies taut to the heat. Legs rigid. they lay in running attitudes. like stuffed dogs knocked over on to their sides. On the sofa pulled up opposite the fire was Clifford – feet braced against one end, backbone against the other, knees up, typewriter in the pit of his stomach, chin tucked down into his chest. With elbows in to his ribs in a trussed position, he now and then made a cramped dash at the keys. When the keys stopped, he stayed frowning at them. Sheet after sheet, completed without conviction, fluttered on to the hearthrug between the dogs.

Polly Perry-Dunton's armchair was pushed up so that one arm made telepathic contact with .Clifford's sofa. Curled up childishly in the cushions, she held a Penguin volume a little above her face. She kept the stiff Penguin open by means of an anxious pressure from her thumb. She read like someone told to pose with a book, and seemed unable to read without holding her breath.

Crackles came now and then from the *Daily Sketch* that Clifford had folded under his feet. Light blazed on their two heads from a marble bowl near the ceiling. The top of the mantelpiece was stacked with Penguins; the other armchair was stacked with American magazines. Polly's portable wireless in its shagreen cover stood silent on the floor by her chair. An art photograph of Clifford and Polly, profiles just overlapping like heads on a coin, was propped on the whatnot and kept from slipping by Polly's toy panda from Fortnum's.

Clifford reached out his right hand, apparently vaguely: Polly uncoiled like a spring from the armchair, knelt on the hearthrug and lit him a cigarette. Cigarette pressed tightly between his lips, Clifford turned back to frown at the keys again. She sat back on her heels to adore his frown, his curls, his fresh skin — then she locked her arms tightly around his neck. The impulsive, light little-girlishness of the movement let him still say nothing, not even turn his head.

She said into his cheek: 'May Polly say one thing?'

'Mm-mm.'

'I've left my pussy gloves in the car.'

'Mm-mm . . . You don't want them, do you?'

'No, not indoors. I wouldn't want gloves indoors. But let's remember tomorrow . . . Look, you crumpled one sheet right up. Did you mean to?'

'I meant to.'

Polly reverently uncrumpled the sheet. 'Pity,' she said. 'It's beautifully typed. Do you mean you're *not* going to say all that?'

'No. I'm trying to think of something else.'

'I should think most people could never think of so much that they were even not going to say.'

Clifford waited a minute, then he unfastened Polly's arms from his neck with as little emotion as a woman un-doing a boa. He then typed five or six lines in a sort of rush. She returned with a glutted sigh to her chair, thumbed her book, held her breath and thought of her pussy gloves.

Clifford's voice to Polly was always the same: resigna-tion or irony kept it on one note. The two of them had been over here on honeymoon when the war began; here they still were, because of the war. Some days he went out with his gun along the foot of the mountain, some days they ran the motor-boat in and out of white inlets or to an island, some days they went out in Polly's big car. When they had run the car back into the lock-up they would walk back, her hand creeping inside his, down the tarmac curve to the hotel between walls of evergreen. At this hour, the tarmac gleamed wet-white in the lasting luminous Irish dusk. From this hour, claustrophobia resumed its sway. Polly hardly reached up to Clifford's shoulders; she walked beside him with her little skip-and-jump. She felt that his being so tall, she so little, cancelled out their adverse difference in age. She was thirty-two, he twenty-four. Her trim little sexless figure, her kilted skirts, socks and little-girl snooded hair that flopped forward so softly could make her look fourteen. Without the ring of technicians who got her up she could have easily looked faded and sluttish, like a little girl in Woolworth's wilting behind the goods. But she had a childish hard will, and by day she never looked old.

She grew up when she was asleep. Then, a map of unwilling adult awareness — lines, tensions and hollows — appeared in her exposed face. Harsh sleep froze her liquidity; her features assembled themselves and became austere. An expression of watching wrote itself on the lids of her shut eyes. The dread she denied all day came out while she slept and stood in the door. The flittering of a palm tree, the bump of a moored boat as the tide rose, the collapse of a last coal in their grate went straight to the nerves upright under her sleep. She slept tenaciously, late into the daylight — but Clifford never looked at her long.

Her rape of Clifford — with his animal muteness, nonchalance, mystery and the charm of the obstination of his wish to write — had been the climax of Polly's first real wish. Her will had detected the flaw in his will that made the bid possible. Her father had bought him for her. Till they met, her wealth and her years of styleless, backgroundless dullness had atrophied Polly. The impulse with which she first put her arms round Clifford's neck and told him never to leave her had been, however, unforced and pure. Rain — a little rain, not much — fell on her small parched nature at Clifford's tentative kiss. There had seemed no threat to Polly in Clifford's nature till the war came, with its masculine threat. Their sequestration now, here, remained outwardly simple: Clifford handled no money, Polly drew all the cheques.

They stayed on here where they were hidden and easy — any move might end in some fatal way. The Perry-

Duntons knew almost nothing of the hotel. They had meals served in their suite, and only went down or upstairs or through the lounge on their way outdoors or in. During such appearances, Polly's service-flat temperament sheathed her in passive, moronic unseeingness. Her blindness made everything negative – Clifford saw nothing, either. He walked out or in through the public rooms beside her, tense, persecuted by the idea of notice, with his baited, defensive frown. The hotel had come to return the Perry-Duntons' indifference. The out-of-season skeleton staff of servants served them without interest, acting the automata Polly took them to be. Servants love love and money, but the Perry-Duntons bored the servants, by now. By now even Mrs Coughlan, the manageress, thought and spoke of them with apathy. The Perry-Duntons deadened the air round them with their static depleting intimacy.

Now, Clifford twitched one more sheet off the machine. Leaning sideways over from the sofa, he, with absorption, began to tickle a dog's belly with an edge of the sheet. The dog bent itself further backward, into a bow. Watchful, Polly judged that this meant a break. She got up and began to tug like a bird at the *Daily Sketch* under Clifford's feet. 'What's that there for?' she said. 'I don't think I've looked at it yet.'

'Sorry,' said Clifford, raising his feet.

'But what's it *there* for, Clifford?'

'I was taught not to put my boots up on things. – not straight up on things, that is.'

'How funny, because you generally do. I wonder what made you just think of that?'

Clifford could not tell her. He swung his feet off the sofa on to the hearthrug between the dogs. Sitting forward on the edge of the sofa, elbows on his wide-apart knees, he dug his heels slowly, without passion, into the rug. He looked slowly down from his hands with their hanging bunches of fingers to the oriental pattern under them. Polly picked up a sheet of typewriting and began to read.

'Goodness,' she said, after an interval, 'I hope you're not going to *throw* this one away! ... What's the matter?'

'I'm going out for your gloves.'

'Oh, but I don't want them.'

'I'd like to go out for them, rather. I'd like a stretch.'

'*Alone*, Clifford?'

'There's a mist.'

'You might get lost. You might walk into the water. Do you really *want* to go out?'

At this, the dogs got up and looked eager. He pushed at them with his feet. 'No, stay with Polly,' he said. 'I won't be long.'

'You do promise?' She folded herself away from him in an abandon of puzzled sadness. Clifford kicked the dogs back again and went quietly round the door.

Frank stepped across the corridor to the office to get a stamp for Linda. The plate-glass and mahogany front of the office was framed in tariffs of summer trips, sets of view postcards printed in dark blue and a bill of the working hours of the Protestant church. The glass hatch was down: Frank put his face against it and looked flirtatiously into the back recess. On an inside ledge, the register was just out of view. Mrs. Coughlan put up the glass hatch, like a lady playing at keeping shop. She received the full blast of Frank's full-blooded charm. 'Stamp?' she said. 'Oh dear, now, Miss Heally knows where they are. To tell you the truth, I'm afraid I don't, and Miss Heally's just upstairs having a little rest. We're very quiet just now. Don't you find it terribly quiet – Major Mull?'

'Mr. Mull,' said Frank. 'Oh, we love it,' he said.

'Still, it's not like the season, is it? Will you be back with us then?'

'Will I not!' said Frank, using his eyes.

'Is the stamp for yourself?'

'Well, it's not: it's for my cousin.'

'Ah yes,' said Mrs. Coughlan, not batting an eyelid. The post went, you know; it went about five minutes. But I tell you what – Were you never in the last war?' – 'I was,' said Frank. 'But I'm not in this one, thank God.' – 'Now Miss Heally thought you had some military rank – I tell you what I could do, I could let you have a stamp I have, if I could trouble you to step this way.'

She pressed with her corsets against the door of the counter, and Frank let her out. She preceded him down the warm, half-lit, spongey-carpeted corridor to the door of her sitting-room: from this, she recoiled on to Frank's toe, at the same time blowing a whisper in at his right ear. 'I won't ask you in here,' she said 'if you don't mind. I've a lady in here who is a little upset.' As she spoke, the door of the sitting-room opened, and the, to Frank's eye, snappy form of Teresa appeared, outlined in electric light. Teresa glowered at Frank, then said: 'We'll be going now, Mrs. Coughlan. I think my mother would really rather be home.'

'I would not rather!' exclaimed unseen Mrs. Massey. 'For God's sake, Teresa, let me alone.'

'No, don't let me barge in,' said Frank, standing firmly just where he was. Mrs. Coughlan flashed at him the recognition that *he* would be always the gentleman. 'Well, if you'll excuse me,' she said, 'for just a jiffy, I'll bring the stamp along to your sittingroom.'

Frank went back to Linda. He left their door an inch open and, while they were waiting, rang for a glass of port. 'What's that for?' said Linda. 'I wanted a stamp.'

'That's for Mrs. Coughlan. You'll get your stamp to play with. But of course you know that the post's gone?' 'Then hell, what is the good of a stamp?' 'You said you wanted a stamp, so I'm getting a stamp for you. I love getting you anything that you want.' 'Then what's the point of me having written this letter?' 'None, darling; I told you that. Writing letters is just fidgets. Never mind, it will come in some time when you want a letter to post.'

Disengaging herself from Frank's kiss, Linda propped the letter up on the mantelpiece, on a carton of cigarettes. While he kissed her again, she looked at it out of one eye.

This made Frank look too. 'Oh, *that's* who it's to,' he said. He made faces at it, while Linda, still held pressed to his chest, giggled contentedly. 'I sort of had to,' she said, 'or he wouldn't know where I am.'

Mrs. Coughlan came in with the stamp. The port was brought in by Michael and put on the mantelpiece. She started at it, but after a certain amount of fuss was induced to life her glass daintily. 'Well, here's to you' she said. 'And to you too,' she said to Linda. 'But isn't this really dreadful, at this hour.'

'Good for the heart,' said Frank. 'Not that your heart needs it, I'm sure. But your caller sounded to me a bit off.'

'Oh, Mrs. Massey's had bad news. She came round here with her daughter, then didn't feel well.'

'Was she in the lounge?' said Linda.

'She was first, but it didn't seem fit for her, so Miss Teresa made her come in to me. You don't know who might come into a public room. So I said, to come in to me for a little rest, while I kept an eye on the office while Miss Heally was up. We are all devoted to Mrs. Massey,' said Mrs. Coughlan, meeting the eye of Linda just a shade stonily. 'I was saying to Miss Heally only this morning, wasn't it too long since we'd seen Teresa or her. They're in and out, as a rule, with the friends Mrs. Massey has staying. They're quite near to here, through the woods, though it's longer if you take the two avenues. They've a sweet place, there, but it's lonely; they've nothing there but the sea.'

'Through the woods?' said Linda. 'Then, do you mean that pink house? – That's that house *we* want,' she said to Frank. Mrs. Coughlan glanced primly midway between the two of them. 'Yes, it's a sweet place, Palmlawn,' said Mrs. Coughlan. 'We often say, she seems quite wedded to it.'

Frank said: 'Is Teresa the tiger cat?'

Far too much won by Frank's eye and manner, Mrs. Coughlan had to pause to prop up her loyalties, 'Well, her manner's just a weeshy bit short,' she said. 'And this evening, of course, *she's* upset, too.'

'She sounded more fed up.'

Mrs. Coughlan, replacing her glass on the mantelpiece, dabbed her mouth with an *eau de nil* handkerchief charged with *Muguet de Coty*. Reassembling herself as manageress, she threw an inventorial glance round their sitting-room. 'I hope,' she said, 'you have everything? Everything comfy? Ring if it isn't, won't you?' 'Yes, thanks,' said Linda, 'we're very cosy in here.' Mrs. Coughlan, whose business it was to know how to take everything, knew perfectly well how to take this. 'Well, I must be running along. Thank you very much, Major Mull – Mr. Mull – I hope you'll join *me* for a minute or two this evening, unless, of course, you're engaged . . . Isn't this war shocking?'

'Shocking,' said Frank. 'I sell cars.'

'Very,' said Linda. 'Why?'

'I can't help thinking,' said Mrs. Coughlan, 'of poor Mrs. Massey's friend. A flying man. He was often in here, you know.'

Fumbling with the slimy lock in the mist, Clifford unlocked the lock-up. He reached into the Alvis, switched the dashboard lights on and got in and sat in the car to look for Polly's gloves. Mist came curdling into the lock-up after him. He put the wristlength, fluffy gloves in one pocket. Then he checked up on the petrol: there were six gallons still. Then he plunged his hand slowly into another of his pockets, touched the pennies, thumbed the two half-crowns. In the dark his body recorded, not for the first time, yet another shock of the recurrent idea. The shock, as always, dulled out. He switched the lights off, folded his arms, slid forward and sat in the dark deflated – completely deflated, a dying pig that has died.

Frank and Linda, intently, silently cosy in front of their sitting-room fire in the dark, heard people break into the passage from Mrs. Coughlan's room. At this Frank, with pussy-cat stealth and quickness, raised his face from the top of Linda's head. His clean ears, close to his head, might have been said to prick up. 'Damn,' said Linda, missing Frank, 'something is always happening.' The concourse passed their door. 'That's Mrs. Massey, that was.' Frank at once pressed his hands on Linda's shoulders. But he said: 'Should I just have a look-see?' He got up, padded across the room, opened the door an inch and put one eye to the inch.

Mrs. Coughlan had not gone far. She immediately came back and put her mouth into the inch of door. 'Mr. Mull, could I trouble you just a minute?' she said. Frank edged round the door and Linda was left alone.

Mrs. Massey was not equal to the walk back. This — only felt by herself as an additional rush of sorrow — was clear to Teresa, and also to Mrs. Coughlan, as a predicament. There had been talk, before they left Mrs. Coughlan's parlour, of telephoning to the village for a car. Mrs. Massey would not brook the idea. 'I won't give trouble,' she said. 'There's trouble enough already.' Magnificent with protest, she now stood trembling and talking loudly and sweeping her hair back at the foot of the stairs. 'I should never have come,' she said. 'But how could I stay where I was? We'll go home now; we'll just go quietly home — Are you gummed there, Teresa? Come home: we've been here quite long enough.' She gave Frank a haunted look as Mrs. Coughlan brought him up. 'This is Mr. Mull, Mrs. Massey,' said Mrs. Coughlan, 'Mr. Mull says he'll just get his car out and run you home.'

Mrs. Massey said: 'I don't know what you all think.'

Teresa, taking no notice, put on her trenchcoat and tightly buckled the belt. 'That is good of you,' she said to Frank slightingly. 'Aren't you busy?' 'Not in the world,' said Frank. 'Hold on while I get the car round.'

'You needn't do that, thank you: Mother and I can walk as far as the car.'

Teresa and Frank, with Mrs. Massey between them, started off down the aisle of carpet to the glass doors. 'Aren't the steps dreadfully dark for her!' yelped Miss Heally, who was there with the rest — she shot ahead to switch on the outdoor lamps. The three passed down the steps in the blur of a blaze of lights, as though leaving a ball. 'Good night now. Safe home, Mrs. Massey dear!' called Miss Heally and Mrs. Coughlan from the top of the steps. Linda, hearing the noise, hearing Frank's step on the gravel, threw a window up and leaned into the mist. She called: 'Frank?' He replied if at all, with a gesture that she could not see: he was busy steering the party. 'Left turn,' he said, patting at Mrs. Massey's elbow. The mother and daughter wheeled docilely.

'Do you know where we are, at all?'

'Oh, I'm used to all this.'

'Do you come from London, then?' Teresa said.

'I've come back from London.'

'On leave?' said Teresa quickly.

'No, thank God. I sell cars.'

'You won't sell many just now.' Teresa's trenchcoat brushed on the evergreens. Majestic and dazed between her escort, Mrs. Massey stumbled along in a shackled way. In the yard, the open doors of the lock-up beside Frank's stuck out clammy into the mist: they almost walked into them. 'That lunatic's taken that Alvis out,' said Frank. Teresa, in her not encouraging way, said: 'Well, you'll be another lunatic, in a minute.' Mrs. Massey, ignoring the dialogue, detached herself quietly from Teresa. While Frank and his torch and key were busy over a padlock, Mrs. Massey passed quietly into the open lock-up next door. She bumped her knee on the Alvis and started to climb round it. 'It's all right, Teresa, the car's in here,' she called back, with quite an approach to her usual gaiety.

Clifford's reflex to the bump on the car was to blaze all his lights on. Inside, his lock-up became one curdled glare; his tail light spread a ruby stain on the mist. He turned his head sharply and stayed with his coinlike profile immobilised against the glaring end wall. Mrs. Massey came scrambling into view. Clifford put down one window. 'I beg your pardon?' he said.

'Better back out a little,' said Mrs. Massey. 'I can't get in this side while you're in here.' Clifford started his engine and backed out. But then he pulled up, got up and got half out of the car. 'I'm afraid this is not your car,' he said

'How could it be my car,' said Mrs. Massey, 'when my car's at home? This is so kind of you – I don't know what you must think. Let me in now, though.' Clifford shrank back; she got in and settled herself by him contentedly. 'There's my daughter to come,' she said, 'and a man from the hotel. Just wait, now, and they'll show you the way.'

Frank had only just got his lock-up open when Teresa was at his elbow again. 'We'll hang on a minute,' he said, 'and let this other chap out. I'll start up. Be getting your mother in at the back.'

'My mother's got into the other car.'

'Which car?'

'I don't know. Don't dawdle there – are you mad? Mother might be off anywhere!'

Frank went out to blink. The Alvis, almost silently turning, swept a choked glare through the mist. 'Oh, *that* chap,' Frank said. 'That chap won't eat anyone. Cut along, Teresa – look, he's waiting for you.'

'I don't know him.'

'Mother knows him by now.'

'You're well out of us,' said Teresa, standing still bitterly.

'If that's what you think,' Frank said, 'I'll come along too.'

Linda was told of Frank's kindness in volunteering to drive the Masseys home. Mrs. Coughlan was very much pleased and could not praise him enough. He should be back at the hotel in twenty minutes – but Linda knew he would not be. Frank's superabundance of good feeling made Linda pretty cross – his gusto, his sociability, his human fun, and his conquering bossiness. He liked life, and wherever he was things happened. This evening, first Mrs. Coughlan, now Mrs. Massey . . . Except in bed, one was seldom alone with Frank. Having interfered once more, and got one more kind act in, he would come back like a cat full of rabbit again. Linda felt quite suspended. She

wished there were pin tables in this high-class hotel. She
rang for a drink and two packs of cards and sat down and
laid out a complex patience on the octagonal table below
the sitting-room light. She thanked God she was not as
young as she had been and no longer fell into desperations
or piques. It was not that Frank did not concentrate, but he
did not concentrate consecutively. She looked up once
from her patience at her stamped letter, and half thought of
tearing it up and writing a warmer one.

Mrs. Coughlan and Miss Heally returned to their sitting-
room; opening the piano they began to play a duet.

Polly Perry-Dunton, as well as Linda, heard the piano.
Every three minutes Polly looked at her watch. After ten
minutes, Polly left her sitting-room and went and lay on
her bed in a sort of rigor. She pulled Clifford's pyjamas out
from under the pillow and buried her face in them.

The Alvis, dip lights squinting along the row of sticky
trees on the left, nosed its way through the mist down the
avenue. Mrs. Massey, in absolute quiescence, leaned back
by Clifford's shoulder: he drove in silence. Frank, in the
back of the car beside Teresa, had noncommittally drawn
her arm through his. Teresa did not take her eyes from the
back of her mother's head. When the open white gates
loomed up, Teresa leaned forward and told Clifford which
way to turn. About a mile down the main road Teresa
again spoke up. Clifford turned through more gates, and
the four of them passed with well-sprung smoothness over
the bumps of a peaty wet avenue. An uneasy smell of the
sea came up the mist. Rhododendrons lolled and brushed
the sides of the car. The left wheels mounted an edge of
lawn. Clifford took a sweep and undipped his lights on
veranda posts and pallid walls of a house.

'Teresa,' said Mrs. Massey, 'tell them to come in.'

Teresa lit the two oil lamps under their dark pink shades.
Mrs. Massey, one hand on her drawing-room mantelpiece,
swayed with the noble naturalness of a tree. Her form,
above a smoulder of peat fire, was reflected in a mirror
between the two dark windows – a mirror that ran from

ceiling, to floor. The room with its possessions, its air of bravura and slipshod moodiness, its low, smoked ceiling, armchairs with sunk seats, cabinets of dull glass began to be seen in the dark light. Clifford's scraggy Nordic figure, and Frank's thick-set springy figure, firmly poised on its heels, were also seen in the mirror, making a crown.

'Sit down,' said Mrs. Massey, 'I feel more like standing. I'm afraid I'm restless – I had bad news, you know.'

'That is frightfully tough,' said Frank.

'I feel bad,' said Mrs. Massey, 'at not knowing your names. Yes, it's tough to be dead isn't it? He was about your age,' she said to Clifford. ' – Teresa dear, are you gummed there? Go and look for the drinks.'

Through the shadows in which they were all still standing up, Clifford threw a quick, begging look at Frank. Frank had to defer to Clifford's panic, and to Clifford's being unable to speak. 'Look, we must be pushing along,' Frank reluctantly, firmly said. Clifford bowed his heroic head sharply and took two steps to the door: the nightmare of being wanted was beginning, in this room, to close in round him again.

Mrs. Massey only removed her eyes from Clifford to attend to a cigarette she was lighting over a lamp. Obliterated in shadows round the unglowing fire, Teresa, crouching, puffed at peat with a bellows. 'Teresa,' said her mother, 'do *you* see who he's so like – ?'

' – There's no drink left, as you know,' said Teresa quickly. 'I could make some tea, but they're just off.'

Clifford said: 'I'm afraid we *are* just off!'

In reply, Mrs. Massey lifted the lamp from its low table to hold it, unsteadily, on a level with Clifford's face. She took a step or two forward, with the lamp. 'It's extraordinary,' she said, 'though you don't know it, that you should be in this house *tonight*. You mustn't mind what I say or do: I'm upset – you're English, too, aren't you? He looks like a hero, doesn't he?' she said appealingly to Frank.

'Now we've all had a look at each other,' said Frank

51

firmly, 'let me take this out of your way.' Taking the wobbling lamp from Mrs. Massey, he put it safely back on its table again.

'I wish I were proud of my country,' said Mrs. Massey. 'But I'm ashamed of this country to tell you the truth.'

'Oh, come,' said Frank. 'We have much to be thankful for.'

Teresa crashed the bellows into the grate and went out of the room through the open door. Outside, she pulled up a chair and stood on it to light the lamp in the hall. Frank strolled after her and leaned in the door to watch. He said: 'Are you very fed up?' The hanging lamp spun round, and Teresa's eyes, fixed on the burner, glittered. 'Is it bad?' Frank said. 'You don't tell me anything. Did *you* love the poor chap?'

'Did I get a chance?'

The chair she stood on wobbled on the uneven flagstones: Frank came and stood close up to steady the chair. 'Come down off that,' he said, 'like a good girl.' Teresa stepped down off the chair into Frank's arms – but she stood inside them like steel. He let her go, and watched her pick up her trenchcoat and walk off down a stone passage to hang it up. There she stayed, as though she were falling and could fall no further, with her breast and face thrust into the hanging coats. Her shoulder-blades showed through her sweater, and Frank, coming up gently, put his two hands on them. 'She'd rather him dead,' said Teresa into the coats, 'she'd rather him dead than gone from her.' She kept moving her shoulders under Frank's hands.

'Could you cry? Could you have a cry if I took you off now in that car?'

Teresa, into the coats, said something he could not hear. 'And leave those two?' she said in a louder voice.

Frank had to agree: he looked back at the drawing-room door.

Mrs. Massey and Clifford waiting for Frank, now sat in two armchairs opposite the fire. 'I don't understand,' she said. 'How did we come in your car?'

'You got in . . .' he said tentatively.

'And where had you been going?'

'Nowhere; I was looking for my wife's gloves. He pulled the pussy gloves out of his pocket and showed them, to show he spoke the truth. Looking intently at the pussy gloves, Mrs. Massey's eyes for the first time filled with tears. The access of some new feeling, a feeling with no context, resculptured her face. In the musty dark of her drawing-room, the dark round the dull fire, her new face looked alabaster and pure. The outline of her mist-clotted fair hair shook, as though shaken by the unconscious silent force of her tears.

'Aren't they small!' she said. 'Is your wife quite a little thing? Are you two very happy, then?'

'Very.'

'Take her gloves back safe . . . How English you are.'

Frank came in and said they must be pushing along. Teresa did not come in; she was opening the hall door. Out there on the sweep above the lawn and the sea, Clifford's lights were still blazing into the mist. Teresa went out and examined, as much by touch as anything, the wonderful car. An idea of going away for ever lifted and moved her heart, like a tide coming in. A whiteness up in the mist showed where there should have been the moon; the sleep-locked sea of the bay sighed. A smell of fern-rot and sea-water and gravel passed by Teresa into the house. Frank came to the hall door and saw her in the mist close to the car. He thought, calmly, of Linda wondering where he was, and wanted to go, and wanted to stay, and conceived how foolish it was, in love, to have to differentiate between women. In love there is no right and wrong, only the wish. However, he left Teresa alone and, going back into the drawing-room, said something further to Clifford about dinner.

Mrs. Massey was just detaching her arms from Clifford's neck. 'I had to kiss him,' she said. 'He'll never understand why.' She went slowly ahead of the two men out to the car. 'Dinner?' she said. 'Is that really what time it is? . . .

53

Teresa?'

But there was no reply.

Up the mist between the formless rhododendrons the Alvis, with Frank and Clifford, crawled back to the main road. 'If you thought of turning this car in before leaving this country,' Frank said, 'you might let me know first? My name's Mull – Mull, Cork always finds me.'

'My name is Perry-Dunton,' said Clifford, after a pause.

'Yes, I thought it might be.'

'Why?' said Clifford, alarmed.

'Caught my eye on the register. You two seem to like it here. And how right you are. Staying on?'

'Well, we're not quite sure of our plans.'

'I wish I wasn't – we've only got the week-end. Look, why don't you two drop down for a drink with us after dinner? My cousin would be delighted.'

'It is most awfully kind of you, but I don't think –'

'Right-o,' said Frank, nodding his head.

Unwelcome Idea

Along Dublin Bay, on a sunny July morning, the public gardens along the Dalkey tramline look bright as a series of parasols. Chalk-blue sea appears at the ends of the roads of villas turning downhill — but these are still the suburbs, not the seaside. In the distance, floating across the bay, buildings glitter out of the heat-haze on the neck to Howth, and Howth Head looks higher veiled. After inland Ballsbridge, the tram from Dublin speeds up; it zooms through the residential reaches with the gathering steadiness of a launched ship. Its red velvet seating accommodation is seldom crowded — its rival, the quicker bus, lurches ahead of it down the same road.

After Ballsbridge, the ozone smell of the bay sifts more and more through the smell of chimneys and pollen and the July-darkened garden trees as the bay and line converge. Then at a point you see the whole bay open — there are nothing but flats of grass and the sunk railway between the running tram and the still sea. An immense glaring reflection floods through the tram. When high terraces, backs to the tramline, shut out the view again, even their backs have a salted, marine air: their cotton window-blinds are pulled half down, crooked; here and there an inner door left open lets you see a flash of sea through a house. The weathered lions on gate posts ought to be dolphins. Red, low-lying villas have been fitted between earlier terraces, ornate, shabby, glassy hotels, bow-fronted mansions all built in the first place to stand up over spaces of grass. Looks from trams and voices from public gardens invade the old walled lawns with their grottos and weeping willows. Spit-and-polish alternates with decay. But stucco, slate and slate-fronts, blotched Italian pink-wash, dusty windows, lace curtains and dolphin-lions seem to be the eternity of this tram route. Quite soon the modern will sag, chip, fade. Change leaves everything at the same level. Nothing stays bright but mornings.

The tram slides to stops for its not many passengers. The Blackrock bottleneck checks it, then the Dun Laoghaire. These are the shopping centres strung on the line: their animation congests them. Housewives with burnt bare arms out of their cotton dresses mass blinking and talking among the halted traffic, knocking their shopping-bags on each other's thighs. Forgotten Protestant ladies from 'rooms' near the esplanade stand squeezed between the kerb and the shops. A file of booted children threads its way through the crush, a nun at the head like a needle. Children by themselves curl their toes in their plimsolls and suck sweets and disregard everything. The goods stacked in the shops look very static and hot. Out from the tops of the shops on brackets stand a number of clocks. As though wrought up by the clocks the tram-driver smites his bell again and again, till the checked tram noses its way through.

By half-past eleven this morning one tram to Dalkey is not far on its way. All the time it approaches the Balls-bridge stop Mrs. Kearney looks undecided, but when it does pull up she steps aboard because she has seen no bus. In a slither of rather ungirt parcels, including a dress-box, with a magazine held firmly between her teeth, she clutches her way up the stairs to the top. She settles herself on a velvet seat: she is hot. But the doors at each end and the windows are half-open, and as the tram moves air rushes smoothly through. There are only four people and no man smokes a pipe. Mrs. Kearney has finished wedging her parcels between her hip and the side of the tram and is intending to look at her magazine when she stares hard ahead and shows interest in someone's back. She moves herself and everything three seats up, leans forward and gives a poke at the back. 'Isn't that you?' she says.

Miss Kevin jumps round so wholeheartedly that the brims of the two hats almost clash. 'Why, for goodness' sake! . . . Are you on the tram?' She settled round in her seat with her elbow hooked over the back – it is bare and sharp, with a rubbed joint: she and Mrs. Kearney are of an age, and the age is about thirty-five. They both wear printed dresses that in this weather stick close to their backs; they are enthusiastic, not close friends but as close as they are ever likely to be. They both have high, fresh, pink colouring; Mrs. Kearney could do with a little less weight and Miss Kevin could do with a little more.

They agree they are out early. Miss Kevin has been in town for the July sales but is now due home to let her mother go out. She has parcels with her but they are compact and shiny, having been made up at the counters of shops. 'They all say, buy now. You never know.' She cannot help looking at Mrs. Kearney's parcels, bursting out from their string. 'And aren't you very laden, also.' she says.

'I tell you what I've been doing,' says Mrs. Kearney. 'I've been saying goodbye to my sister Maureen in Balls-bridge, and who knows how long it's to be for! My sister's off to County Cavan this morning with the whole of her family and the maid.'

'For goodness' sake,' says Miss Kevin. 'Has she relatives there?'

'She has, but it's not that. She's evacuating. For the holidays they always go to Tramore, but this year she says she should evacuate.' This brings Mrs. Kearney's parcels into the picture. 'So she asked me to keep a few of her things for her.' She does not add that Maureen has given her these old things, including the month-old magazine.

'Isn't it well for her,' says Miss Kevin politely. 'But won't she find it terribly slow down there?'

'She will, I tell you,' says Mrs. Kearney. 'However, they're all driving down in the car. She's full of it. She says we should all go somewhere where we don't live. It's nothing to her to shift when she has the motor. But the latest thing I hear they say now in the paper is that we'll be shot if we don't stay where we are. They say now we're all to keep off the roads — and there's my sister this morning with her car at the door. Do you think they'll halt her, Miss Kevin?'

'They might,' says Miss Kevin. 'I hear they're very suspicious. I declare, with the instructions changing so quickly it's better to take no notice. You'd be upside down if you tried to follow them all. It's of the first importance to keep calm, they say, and however would we keep calm doing this, then that? Still, we don't get half the instructions they get in England. I should think they'd really pity themselves. . . . Have you earth in your house, Mrs. Kearney? We have, we have three buckets. The warden's delighted with us: he says we're models. We haven't a refuge, though. Have you one?'

'We have a kind of pump, but I don't know it is much good. And nothing would satisfy Fergus till he turned out the cellar.'

'Well, you're very fashionable!'

'The contents are on the lawn, and the lawn's ruined. He's crazy,' she says glumly, 'with A.R.P.'

'Aren't men very thorough,' says Miss Kevin with a virgin detachment that is rather annoying. She has kept thumbing her sales parcels, and now she cannot resist undoing one. 'Listen,' she says, 'isn't this a pretty delaine?' She runs the end of a fold between her finger and thumb. 'It drapes sweetly. I've enough for a dress and a bolero. It's French: they say we won't get any more now.'

'And that Coty scent — isn't that French?'

Their faces flood with the glare struck from the sea as the tram zooms smoothly along the open reach — wall and trees on its inland side, grass and bay on the other. The tips of their shingles and the thoughts in their heads are for the minute blown about and refreshed. Mrs. Kearney flutters in the holiday breeze, but Miss Kevin is looking inside her purse. Mrs. Kearney thinks she will take the kids to the strand. 'Are you a great swimmer, Miss Kevin?'

'I don't care for it: I've a bad circulation. It's a fright to see me go blue. They say now the sea's full of mines,' she says, with a look at the great, innocent bay.

'Ah, they're tethered; they'd never bump you.'

'I'm not nervous at any time, but I take a terrible chill.'

'My sister Maureen's nervous. At Tramore she'll never approach the water: it's the plage she enjoys. I wonder what will she do if they stop the car — she has all her plate with her in the back with the maid. And her kiddies are very nervous: they'd never stand it. I wish now I'd asked her to send me a telegram. Or should I telegraph her to know did she arrive? . . . Wasn't it you said we had to keep off the roads?'

'That's in the event of invasion, Mrs. Kearney. In the event of not it's correct to evacuate.'

'She's correct all right, then,' says Mrs. Kearney, with a momentary return to gloom. 'And if nothing's up by the finish she'll say she went for the holiday, and I shouldn't wonder if she still went to Tramore. Still, I'm sure I'm greatly relieved to hear what you say. . . . Is that your father's opinion?'

Miss Kevin becomes rather pettish. 'Him?' she says, 'oh gracious, I'd never ask him. He has a great contempt for the whole war. My mother and I daren't refer to it — isn't it very mean of him? He does nothing but read the papers and roar away to himself. And will he let my mother or me near him when he has the news on? You'd think,' Miss Kevin says with a clear laugh, 'that the two of us originated the war to spite him: he doesn't seem to blame Hitler at all. He's really very unreasonable when he's not well. We'd a great fight to get in the buckets of earth, and now he makes out they're only there for the cat. And to hear the warden praising us makes him sour. Isn't it very mean to want us out of it all, when they say the whole of the country is drawn together? He doesn't take any pleasure in A.R.P.'

'To tell you the truth I don't either,' says Mrs. Kearney. 'Isn't it that stopped Horse Show? Wouldn't that take the heart out of you – isn't that a great blow to national life? I never yet missed a Horse Show – Sheila was nearly born there. And isn't that a terrible blow to trade? I haven't the heart to look for a new hat. To my mind this war's getting very monotonous: all the interest of it is confined to a few. . . . Did you go to the Red Cross Fête?'

The tram grinds to a halt in Dun Laoghaire Street. Simultaneously Miss Kevin and Mrs. Kearney move up to the window ends of their seats and look closely down on the shop windows and shoppers. Town heat comes off the street in a quiver and begins to pervade the immobile tram. 'I declare to goodness,' exclaims Miss Kevin, 'there's my same delaine! French, indeed! And watch the figure it's on – it would sicken you.'

But with parallel indignation Mrs. Kearney has just noticed a clock. "Will you look at the time!' she says, plaintively. 'Isn't this an awfully slow tram! There's my morning gone, and not a thing touched at home, from attending evacuations. It's well for her! She expected me on her step by ten – "It's a terrible parting," she says on the p.c. But all she does at the last is to chuck the parcels at me, then keep me running to see had they the luncheon basket and what had they done with her fur coat. . . . I'll be off at the next stop, Miss Kevin dear. Will you tell your father and mother I was inquiring for them?' Crimson again at the very notion of moving, she begins to scrape her parcels under her wing. 'Well,' she says, 'I'm off with the *objets d'art*.' The heels of a pair of evening slippers protrude from a gap at the end of the dress box. The tram-driver, by smiting his bell, drowns any remark Miss Kevin could put out: the tram clears the crowd and moves down Dun Laoghaire Street, between high flights of steps, lace curtains, gardens with round beds. 'Bye-bye, now,' says Mrs. Kearney, rising and swaying.

'Bye-bye to you,' said Miss Kevin. 'Happy days to us all.'

Mrs. Kearney, near the top of the stairs, is preparing to bite on the magazine. 'Go on!' she says. 'I'll be seeing you before then.'

Summer Night

As the sun set its light slowly melted the landscape, till everything was made of fire and glass. Released from the glare of noon, the haycocks now seemed to float on the aftergrass: their freshness penetrated the air. In the not far distant hills with woods up their flanks lay in light like hills in another world – it would be a pleasure of heaven to stand up there, where no foot ever seemed to have trodden, on the spaces between the woods soft as powder dusted over with gold. Against those hills, the burning red rambler roses in cottage gardens along the roadside looked earthy – they were too near the eye.

The road was in Ireland. The light, the air from the distance, the air of evening rushed transversely through the open sides of the car. The rims of the hood flapped, the hood's metal frame rattled as the tourer, in great bounds of speed, held the road's darkening magnetic centre streak. The big shabby family car was empty but for its small driver – its emptiness seemed to levitate it – on its back seat a coat slithered about, and a dressing-case bumped against the seat. The driver did not relax her excited touch on the wheel: now and then while she drove she turned one wrist over, to bring the watch worn on it into view, and she gave the mileage marked on the yellow signposts a flying, jealous, half-inadvertent look. She was driving parallel with the sunset: the sun slowly went down on her right hand.

The hills flowed round till they lay ahead. Where the road bent for its upward course through the pass she pulled up and lighted a cigarette. With a snatch she untwisted her turban; she shook her hair free and threw the scarf behind her into the back seat. The draught of the pass combed her hair into coarse strands as the car hummed up in second gear. Behind one brilliantly outlined crest the sun had now quite gone; on the steeps of bracken, in the electric shadow, each frond stood out and climbing goats turned their heads. The car came up on a lorry, to hang on its tail, impatient, checked by turns of the road. At the first stretch the driver smote her palm on the horn and shot past and shot on ahead again.

The small woman drove with her chin up. Her existence was in her hands on the wheel and in the sole of the foot in which she felt, through the sandal, the throbbing pressure of the accelerator. Her face, enlarged by blown-back hair, was as overbearingly blank as the face of a figurehead; her black eyebrows were ruled level, and her eyes, pupils dilated, did little more than reflect the low burn of daylight along horizons, the luminous shades of the half-dark.

Clear of the pass, approaching the county town, the road widened and straightened between stone walls and burnished, showering beech. The walls broke up into gateways and hoardings and the suburbs began. People in modern building estate gardens let the car in a hurry through their unseeing look. The raised footpaths had margins of grass. White and grey rows of cottages under the pavement-level let woodsmoke over their half-doors: women and old men sat outside the doors on boxes, looking down at their knees; here and there a bird sprang in a cage tacked to a wall. Children chasing balls over the roadway shot whooping right and left of the car. The refreshed town, unfolding streets to its centre, at this hour slowly heightened, cooled; streets and stones threw off a grey-pink glare, sultry lasting ghost of the high noon. In this dayless glare the girls in bright dresses, strolling, looked like colour photography.

Dark behind all the windows: not a light yet. The ingoing perspective looked meaning, noble and wide. But everybody was elsewhere – the polished street was empty but cars packed both the kerbs under the trees. What was going on? The big tourer dribbled, slipped with animal nervousness between the static, locked cars each side of its way. The driver peered left and right with her face narrow, glanced from her wrist watch to the clock in the tower, sucked her lip, manoeuvred for somewhere to pull in. The A.A. sign of the hotel hung out from under a balcony over the steps. She edged in to where it said *Do Not Park.*

At the end of the hotel hall one electric light from the bar shone through a high-up panel: its yellow sifted on to the dusty dusk and a moth could be seen on the glass pane. At the door end came in street daylight, to fall weakly on prints on the oiled walls, on the magenta announcement strip of a cinema, on the mahogany bench near the receptionist's office, on the hatstand with two forgotten hats. The woman who had come breathlessly up the steps felt in her face a wall of indifference. The impetuous click of her heeled sandals on the linoleum brought no one to the receptionist's desk, and the drone of two talkers in the bar behind the glass panel seemed, like the light, to be blotted up, word by word. The little woman attacked the desk with her knuckles. 'Is there nobody there – I say? Is there nobody *there?*'

'I am, I am. Wait now,' said the hotel woman, who came impassively through the door from the bar. She reached up a hand and fumbled the desk light on, and by this with unwondering negligence studied the customer – the childish, blown little woman with wing-like eyebrows and eyes still unfocused after the long road. The hotel woman, bust on the desk, looked down slowly at the bare legs, the crumple-hemmed linen coat. 'Can I do anything for you?' she said, when she had done.

'I want the telephone – want to put through a call!'

'You can of course,' said the unmoved hotel woman. 'Why not?' she added after consideration, handing across the keys of the telephone cabinet. The little woman made a slide for the cabinet: with her mouth to the mouthpiece, like a conspirator, she was urgently putting her number through. She came out then and ordered herself a drink.

'Is it long distance?'

'Mm-mm . . . What's on here? What are all those cars?'

'Oh, this evening's the dog racing.'

'Is it?'

'Yes, it's the dog racing. We'd a crowd in here, but they're all gone on now.'

'I wondered who they were,' said the little woman, her eyes on the cabinet, sippeting at her drink.

'Yes, they're at the dog racing. There's a wonderful crowd. But I wouldn't care for it,' said the hotel woman, fastidiously puckering up her forehead. 'I went the one time, but it didn't fascinate me.'

The other forgot to answer. She turned away with her drink, sat down, put the glass beside her on the mahogany bench and began to chafe the calves of her bare legs as though they were stiff or cold. A man clasping sheets of unfurled newspaper pushed his way with his elbow through the door from the bar. 'What it says here,' he said, shaking the paper with both hands, 'is identically what I've been telling you.'

'That proves nothing,' said the hotel woman. 'However, let it out of your hand.' She drew the sheets of the paper from him and began to fold them into a wad. Her eyes moved like beetles over a top line. 'That's an awful battle . . .'

'What battle?' exclaimed the little woman, stopping rubbing her legs but not looking up.

'An awful air battle. Destroying each other,' the woman added, with a stern and yet voluptuous sigh. 'Listen, would you like to wait in the lounge?'

'She'd be better there,' put in the man who had brought the paper. 'Better accommodation.' His eyes watered slightly in the electric light. The little woman, sitting up-right, abruptly, looked defiantly, as though for the first time, at the two watching her from the desk. 'Mr.

Donovan has great opinions,' said the hotel woman. 'Will you move yourself out of here?' she asked Mr. Donovan. 'This is very confined — *There's* your call, now!'

But the stranger had packed herself into the telephone box like a conjuror's lady preparing to disappear. '*Hullo?*' she was saying. 'Hullo! I want to speak to — '

' — You are,' the other voice cut in. 'All right? Anything wrong?'

Her face flushed all over. 'You sound nearer already! I've got to C——.'

The easy, calm voice said: 'Then you're coming along well.'

'Glad, are you?' she said, in a quiver.

'Don't take it too fast,' he said. 'It's a treacherous light. Be easy, there's a good girl.'

'You're a fine impatient man.' His end of the line was silent. She went on: 'I might stay here and go to the dog racing.'

'Oh, is that tonight?' He went on to say equably (having stopped, as she saw it, and shaken the ash off the tip of his cigarette), 'No, I shouldn't do that.'

'Darling . . .'

'Emma . . . How is the Major?'

'He's all right,' she said, rather defensively.

'I see,' he said. 'Everything quite O.K.?'

'In an hour, I'll be . . . where do you live.'

'First gate on the left. Don't kill yourself, there's a good girl. Nothing's worth that. Remember we've got the night. By the way, where are you talking?'

'From the hotel.' She nursed the receiver up close to her face and made a sound into it. Cutting that off she said: 'Well, I'll hang up. I just . . .'

'Right,' he said — and hung up.

Robinson, having hung up the receiver, walked back from the hall to the living-room where his two guests were. He still wore a smile. The deaf woman at the table by the window was pouring herself out another cup of tea.

'That will be very cold!' Robinson shouted – but she only replaced the cosy with a mysterious smile. 'Let her be,' said her brother. 'Let her alone!'

The room in this uphill house was still light: through the open window came in a smell of stocks from the flower beds in the lawn. The only darkness lay in a belt of beech trees at the other side of the main road. From the grate, from the coal of an unlit fire came the fume of a cigarette burning itself out. Robinson still could not help smiling: he reclaimed his glass from the mantelpiece and slumped back with it into his leather armchair in one of his loose, heavy, good-natured attitudes. But Justin Cavey, in the armchair opposite, still looked crucified at having the talk torn. 'Beastly,' he said, 'you've a beastly telephone.' Though he was in Robinson's house for the first time, his sense of attraction to people was marked, early, by just this intransigence and this fretfulness.

'It is and it's not,' said Robinson. That was that. 'Where had we got to?' he amiably asked.

The deaf woman, turning round from the window, gave the two men, or gave the air between them, a penetrating smile. Her brother, with a sort of lurch at his pocket, pulled out a new packet of cigarettes: ignoring Robinson's held-out cigarette case he frowned and split the cellophane with his thumbnail. But, as though his sister had put a hand on his shoulder, his tension could be almost seen to relax. The impersonal, patient look of the thinker appeared in his eyes, behind the spectacles. Justin was a city man, a black-coat, down here (where his sister lived) on holiday. Other summer holidays before this he had travelled in France, Germany, Italy: he disliked the chaotic 'scenery' of his own land. He was down here with Queenie this summer only because of the war, which had locked him in: duty seemed to him better than failed pleasure. His father had been a doctor in this place; now his sister lived on in two rooms in the square – for fear Justin should not be comfortable she had taken a room for him at the hotel. His holiday with his sister, his holiday in this underwater, weedy region of memory, his holiday on which, almost every day, he had to pass the doors of their old home, threatened Justin with a pressure he could not bear. He had to share with Queenie, as he shared the dolls' house meals cooked on the oil stove behind her sitting-room screen, the solitary and almost fairylike world created by her deafness. Her deafness broke down his only defence, talk. He was exposed to the odd, immune, plumbing looks she was for ever passing over his face. He could not deflect the tilted blue of her eyes. The things she said out of nowhere, things with no surface context, were never quite off the mark. She was not all solicitude; she loved to be teasing him.

In her middle-age Queenie was very pretty: her pointed face had the colouring of an imperceptibly fading pink-and-white sweet-pea. This hot summer her artless dresses, with their little lace collars, were mottled over with flowers, mauve and blue. Up the glaring main street she carried a *poult-de-soie* parasol. Her rather dark first-floor rooms faced north, over the square with its grass and lime trees: the crests of great mountains showed above the opposite façades. She would slip in and out on her own errands, as calm as a cat, and Justin, waiting for her at one of her windows, would see her cross the square in the noon sunshine with hands laced over her forehead into a sort of porch. The little town, though strung on a through road, was an outpost under the mountains: in its quick-talking, bitter society she enjoyed, to a degree that surprised Justin, her privileged place. She was woman enough to like to take the man Justin round with her and display him; they went out to afternoon or to evening tea, and in those drawing-rooms of tinted lace and intently staring family photographs, among octagonal tables and painted cushions, Queenie, with her cotton gloves in her lap, well knew how to contribute, while Justin talked, her airy, brilliant, secretive smiling and looking on. For his part, he was man enough to respond to being shown off — besides, he was eased by these breaks in their *tête-à tête*. Above all, he was glad, for these hours or two of chatter, not to have to face the screen of his own mind, on which the distortion of every one of his images, the war-broken towers of Europe, constantly stood. The immolation of what had been his own intensely had been made, he could only feel, without any choice of his. In the heart of the neutral Irishman indirect suffering pulled like a crooked knife. So he acquiesced to, and devoured, society: among the doctors, the solicitors, the auctioneers, the bank people of this little town he renewed old acquaintanceships and developed new. He was content to bloom, for this settled number of weeks – so unlike was this to his monkish life in the city – in a sort of tenebrous popularity. He attempted to check his solitary arrogance. His celibacy and his studentish manner could still, although he was past forty, make him acceptable as a young man. In the mornings he read late in his hotel bed; he got up to take his solitary walks; he returned to flick at his black shoes with Queenie's duster and set off with Queenie on their tea-table rounds. They had been introduced to Robinson, factory manager, in the hall of the house of the secretary of the tennis club.

Robinson did not frequent drawing-rooms. He had come here only three years ago, and had at first been taken to be a bachelor – he was a married man living apart from his wife. The resentment occasioned by this discovery had been aggravated by Robinson's not noticing it: he worked at very high pressure in his factory office, and in his off times his high-powered car was to be seen streaking too gaily out of the town. When he was met, his imperturbable male personality stood out to the women unpleasingly, and stood out most of all in that married society in which women aspire to break the male in a man. Husbands slipped him in for a drink when they were alone or shut themselves up with him in the dining-room. Justin had already sighted him in the hotel bar. When Robinson showed up, late, at the tennis club, his manner with women was easy and teasing, but abstract and perfectly automatic. From this had probably come the legend that he liked women 'only in one way'. From the first time Justin encountered Robinson, he had felt a sort of anxious, disturbed attraction to the big, fair, smiling, offhand, cold-minded man. He felt impelled by Robinson's unmoved physical presence into all sorts of aberrations of talk and mind; he committed, like someone waving an anxious flag, all sorts of absurdities, as though this type of creature had been a woman; his talk became exaggeratedly cerebral, and he became prone, like a perverse person in love, to expose all his own piques, crotchets and weaknesses. One night in the hotel bar with Robinson he had talked until he burst into tears. Robinson had on him the touch of some foreign sun. The acquaintanceship – it could not be called more – was no more than an accident of this narrowed summer. For Justin it had taken the place of travel. The two men were so far off each other's beat that in a city they would certainly not have met.

Asked to drop in some evening or any evening, the Caveys had tonight taken Robinson at his word. Tonight, the night of the first visit, Justin's high, rather bleak forehead had flushed from the moment he rang the bell. With Queenie behind his shoulder, in muslin, he had flinched confronting the housekeeper. Queenie, like the rest of the town ladies, had done no more till now than go by Robinson's gate.

For her part, Queenie showed herself happy to penetrate into what she had called 'the china house'. On its knoll over the main road, just outside the town, Bellevue did look like china up on a mantelpiece – it was a compact, stucco house with mouldings, recently painted a light blue. From the lawn set with pampas and crescent-shaped flower-beds the hum of Robinson's motor mower passed in summer over the sleepy town. And when winter denuded the trees round them the polished windows, glass porch and empty conservatory sent out, on mornings of frosty sunshine, a rather mischievous and uncaring flash. The almost sensuous cleanness of his dwelling was reproduced in the person of Robinson – about his ears, jaw, collar and close-clipped nails. The approach the Caveys had walked up showed the broad, decided tyre prints of his car.

'Where had we got to?' Robinson said again.

'I was saying we should have to find a new form.'

'Of course you were,' agreed Robinson. 'That was it.' He nodded over the top of Justin's head.

'A new form for thinking and feeling . . .'

'But one thinks what one happens to think, or feels what one happens to feel. That is as just so happens — I should have thought. One either does or one doesn't?'

'One doesn't!' cried Justin. 'That's what I've been getting at. For some time we have neither thought nor felt. Our faculties have slowed down without our knowing — they had stopped without our knowing! We know now. Now that there's enough death to challenge being alive we're facing it that, anyhow, we don't live. We're confronted by the impossiblility *of* living — unless we can break through to something else. There's been a stop in our senses and in our faculties that's made everything round us so much dead matter — and dead matter we couldn't even displace. We can no longer express ourselves: what we say doesn't even approximate to reality; it only approximates to what's been said. I say, this war's an awful illumination; it's destroyed our dark; we have to see where we are. Immobilised, God help us, and each so far apart that we can't even try to signal each other. And our currency's worthless — our "ideas", so on, so on. We've got to mint a new one. We've got to break through to the new form — it needs genius. We're precipitated, this moment, between genius and death. I tell you, we must have genius to live at all.'

'I am certainly dished, then,' said Robinson. He got up and looked for Justin's empty glass and took it to the sideboard where the decanters were.

'We have it!' cried Justin, smiting the arm of his chair. 'I salute your genius, Robinson, but I mistrust my own.'

'That's very nice of you,' said Robinson. 'I agree with you that this war makes one think. I was in the last, but I don't remember thinking: I suppose possibly one had no time. Of course, these days in business one comes up against this war the whole way through. And to tell you the truth,' said Robinson, turning round, 'I do like my off times to *be* my off times, because with this and then that they are precious few. So I don't really think as much as I might – though I see how one might always begin. You don't think thinking gets one a bit rattled?'

'I don't think!' said Justin violently.

'Well, you should know,' said Robinson, looking at his thumbnail. 'I should have thought you did. From the way you talk.'

'I couldn't think if I wanted: I've lost my motivation. I taste the dust in the street and I smell the limes in the square and I beat round inside this beastly shell of the past among images that all the more torment me as they lose any sense that they had. As for feeling –'

'You don't think you find it a bit slow here? Mind you, I haven't a word against this place but it's not a place I'd choose for an off time –'

'– My dear Robinson,' Justin said, in a mincing, schoolmasterish tone, 'You seem blind to our exquisite sociabilities.'

'Pack of old cats,' said Robinson amiably.

'You suggest I should get away for a bit of fun?'

'Well, I did mean that.'

'I find my own fun,' said Justin, 'I'm torn, here, by every single pang of annihilation. But that's what I look for; that's what I want completed; that's the whole of what I want to embrace. On the far side of the nothing – my new form. Scrap "me"; scrap my wretched identity and you'll bring to the open some bud of life. I *not* "I" – I'd be the world ... You're right: what you would call thinking does get me rattled. I only what you call think to excite myself. Take myself away, and I'd *think*. I might see; I might feel purely; I might even love –'

'Fine,' agreed Robinson, not quite easy. He paused and seemed to regard what Justin had just said – at the same time, he threw a glance of perceptible calculation at the electric clock on the mantelpiece. Justin halted and said: 'You give me too much to drink.'

'You feel this war may improve us?' said Robinson.

'What's love like?' Justin said suddenly.

Robinson paused for just less than a second in the act of lighting a cigarette. He uttered a shortish, temporising and, for him, unnaturally loud laugh.

Queenie felt the vibration and turned round, withdrawing her arm from the windowsill. She had been looking intently, between the clumps of pampas, down the lawn to the road: cyclists and walkers on their way into town kept passing Robinson's open gate. Across the road, above the demesne wall, the dark beeches let through glitters of sky, and the colour and scent of the mown lawn and the flowers seemed, by some increase of evening, lifted up to the senses as though a new current flowed underneath. Queenie saw with joy in her own mind what she could not from her place in the window see – the blue china house, with all its reflecting windows, perched on its knoll in the brilliant, fading air. They are too rare – visions of where we are.

When the shock of the laugh made her turn round, she still saw day in Robinson's picture frames and on the chromium fingers of the clock. She looked at Robinson's head, dropped back after the laugh on the leather scroll of his chair: her eyes went from him to Justin. 'Did you two not hit it off?'

Robinson laughed again, this time much more naturally: he emitted a sound like that from inside a furnace in which something is being consumed. Letting his head fall sideways towards Queenie, he seemed to invite her into his mood. 'The way things come out is sometimes funny,' he said to Justin, 'if you know what I mean.'

'No, I don't,' Justin said stonily.

'I bet your sister does.'

'You didn't know what I meant. Anything I may have said about your genius I do absolutely retract.'

'Look here, I'm sorry,' Robinson said, 'I probably took

you up all wrong.'

'On the contrary: the mistake was mine.'

'You know, it's funny about your sister: I never can realise she can't hear. She seems so much one of the party. Would she be fond of children?'

'You mean, why did she not marry?'

'Good God, no – I only had an idea . . .'

Justin went on: 'There was some fellow once, but I never heard more of him. You'd have to be very oncoming, I daresay, to make any way with a deaf girl.'

'No, I meant my children,' said Robinson. He had got up, and he took from his mantelpiece two of the photographs in silver frames. With these he walked down the room to Queenie, who received them with her usual eagerness and immediately turned with them to the light. Justin saw his sister's profile bent forward in study and saw Robinson standing above her leaning against the window frame. When Robinson met an upward look from Queenie he nodded and touched himself on the chest. 'I can see that – aren't they very like you?' she said. He pointed to one picture then held up ten fingers, then to the other and held up eight. 'The fair little fellow's more like you, the bold one. The dark one has more the look of a girl – but he will grow up manly, I daresay . . .' With this she went back to the photographs: she did not seem anxious to give them up, and Robinson made no movement to take them from her – with Queenie the act of looking was always reflective and slow. To Justin the two silhouettes against the window looked wedded and welded by the dark. 'They are both against me,' Justin thought. 'She does not hear with her ears, he does not hear with his mind. No wonder they can communicate.'

'It's a wonder,' she said, 'that you have no little girl.'

Robinson went back for another photograph – but, standing still with a doubtful look at Queenie, he passed his hand, as though sadly expunging something, backwards and forwards across the glass. 'She's quite right; we did have a girl,' he said. 'But I don't know how to tell her the kid's dead.'

Sixty miles away, the Major was making his last round through the orchards before shutting up the house. By this time the bronze-green orchard dusk was intense; the clumped curves of the fruit were hardly to be distinguished among the leaves. The brilliance of evening, in which he had watched Emma driving away, was now gone from the sky. Now and then in the grass his foot knocked a dropped apple – he would sigh, stoop rather stiffly, pick up the apple, examine it with the pad of his thumb for bruises and slip it, tenderly as though it had been an egg, into a baggy pocket of his tweed coat. This was not a good apple year. There was something standardised, uncomplaining about the Major's movements – you saw a tall, unmilitary-looking man with a stoop and a thinnish, drooping moustache. He often wore a slight frown, of doubt or preoccupation. This frown had intensified in the last months.

As he approached the house he heard the wireless talking, and saw one lamp at the distant end of the drawing-room where his aunt sat. At once, the picture broke up – she started, switched off the wireless and ran down the room to the window. You might have thought the room had burst into flames. 'Quick!' she cried. 'Oh, gracious, quick! – I believe it's the telephone.'

The telephone was at the other side of the house – before he got there he heard the bell ringing. He put his hands in his pockets to keep the apples from bumping as he legged it rapidly down the corridor. When he unhooked on his wife's voice he could not help saying haggardly: 'You all right?'

'Of course. I just thought I'd say good night.'

'That was nice of you,' he said, puzzled. 'How is the car running?'

'Like a bird,' she said in a singing voice. 'How are you all?'

'Well, I was just coming in; Aunt Fran's in the drawing-

74

room listening to something on the wireless, and I made the children turn in half an hour ago.'

'You'll go up to them?'

'Yes, I was just going.' For a moment they both paused on the line, then he said: 'Where have you got to now?'

'I'm at T—— now, at the hotel in the square.'

'At T——? Aren't you taking it rather fast?'

'It's a lovely night; it's an empty road.'

'Don't be too hard on the car, she —'

'Oh, I know,' she said, in the singing voice again. 'At C—— I did try to stop, but there was a terrible crowd there: dog racing. So I came on. Darling . . . ?'

'Yes?'

'It's a lovely night, isn't it?'

'Yes, I was really quite sorry to come in. I shall shut up the house now, then go up to the children; then I expect I'll have a word or two with Aunt Fran.'

'I see. Well, I'd better be pushing on.'

'They'll be sitting up for you, won't they?'

'Surely,' said Emma quickly.

'Thank you for ringing up, dear: it was thoughtful of you.'

'I was thinking about you.'

He did not seem to hear this. 'Well, take care of yourself. Have a nice time.'

'Good night,' she said. But the Major had hung up.

In the drawing-room Aunt Fran had not gone back to the wireless. Beside the evening fire lit for her age, she sat rigid, face turned to the door, plucking round and round the rings on her left hand. She wore a foulard dress, net jabot and boned-up collar, of the type ladies wear to dine in private hotels. In the lamplight her waxy features appeared blurred, even effaced. The drawing-room held a crowd of chintz-covered chairs, inlaid tables and wool-worked stools; very little in it was antique, but nothing was strikingly up-to-date. There were cabinets of not rare china, and more blue-and-white plates, in metal clamps, hung in lines up the walls between water-colours. A vase of pink roses arranged by the governess already dropped petals on the piano. In one corner stood a harp with two broken strings – when a door slammed or one made a sudden movement this harp gave out a faint vibration or twang. The silence for miles around this obscure country house seemed to gather inside the folds of the curtains and to dilute the indoor air like a mist. This room Emma liked too little to touch already felt the touch of decay; it threw lifeless reflections into the two mirrors – the walls were green. Aunt Fran's body was stranded here like some object on the bed of a pool that has run dry. The magazine that she had been looking at had slipped from her lap to the black fur rug.

As her nephew appeared in the drawing-room door Aunt Fran fixed him urgently with her eyes. '*Nothing wrong?*'

'No, no – that was Emma.'

'What's happened?'

'Nothing. She rang up to say good night.'

'But she had said good night,' said Aunt Fran in her troubled way. 'She said good night to us when she was in the car. You remember, it was nearly night when she left. It seemed late to be starting to go so far. She had the whole afternoon, but she kept putting off, putting off. She seemed to me undecided up to the very last.'

The Major turned his back on his aunt and began to unload his pockets, carefully placing the apples, two by two, in a row along the chiffonier. 'Still, it's nice for her having this trip,' he said.

'There was a time in the afternoon,' said Aunt Fran, 'when I thought she was going to change her mind. However, she's there now – did you say?'

'Almost,' he said, 'not quite. Will you be all right if I go and shut up the house? And I said I would look in on the girls.'

'Suppose the telephone rings?'

'I don't think it will, again. The exchange will be closing, for one thing.'

'This afternoon,' said Aunt Fran, 'it rang four times.'

She heard him going from room to room, unfolding and barring the heavy shutters and barring and chaining the front door. She could begin to feel calmer now that the house was a fortress against the wakeful night. 'Hi!' she called, 'don't forget the window in here' – looking back over her shoulder into the muslin curtains that seemed to crepitate with dark air. So he came back, with his flat, un-expectant step. 'I'm not cold,' she said, 'but I don't like dark coming in.'

He shuttered the window. 'I'll be down in a minute.'

'Then we might sit together?'

'Yes, Aunt Fran: certainly.'

The children, who had been talking, dropped their voices when they heard their father's step on the stairs. Their two beds creaked as they straightened themselves and lay silent, in social, expectant attitudes. Their room smelled of toothpaste; the white presses blotted slowly into the white walls. The window was open, the blind up, so in here darkness was incomplete – obscured, the sepia picture of the Good Shepherd hung over the mantelpiece. 'It's all right,' they said, 'we are quite awake.' So the Major came round and halted between the two beds. 'Sit on mine,' said Di nonchalantly. 'It's my turn to have a person tonight.'

'Why did Mother ring up?' said Vivie, scrambling up on her pillow.

'Now how on earth did *you* know?'

'We knew by your voice – we couldn't hear what you said. We were only at the top of the stairs. Why did she?'

'To tell me to tell you to be good.'

'She's said that,' said Vivie, impatient. 'What did she say truly?'

'Just good night.'

'Oh. Is she there?'

'Where?'

'Where she said she was going to.'

'Not quite – nearly.'

'Goodness!' Di said; 'it seems years since she went.' The two children lay cryptic and still. Then Di went on: 'Do you know what Aunt Fran said because Mother went away without any stockings?'

'No,' said the Major, 'and never mind.'

'Oh, I don't mind,' Di said, 'I just heard.' 'And I heard,' said Vivie: she could be felt opening her eyes wide, and the Major could just see, on the pillow, an implacable miniature of his wife's face. Di went on: 'She's so frightened something will happen.'

'Aunt Fran is?'

'She's always frightened of that.'

'She is very fond of us all.'

'Oh,' burst out Vivie, 'but Mother likes things to happen. She was whistling all the time she was packing up. Can't *we* have a treat tomorrow?'

'Mother'll be back tomorrow.'

'But *can't* we have a treat?'

'We'll see; we'll ask Mother,' the Major said.

'Oh, yes, but suppose she didn't come back?'

'Look, it's high time you two went to sleep.'

'We can't: we've got all sorts of ideas ... *You* say something, Daddy. Tell us something. Invent.'

'Say what?' said the Major.

'Oh goodness,' Vivie said; '*something*. What do you say to Mother?'

He went downstairs to Aunt Fran with their dissatisfied kisses stamped on his cheek. When he had gone Di fanned herself with the top of her sheet. 'What makes him so disappointed, do you know?'

'I know, he thinks about the war.'

But it was Di who, after the one question, unlocked all over and dropped plumb asleep. It was Vivie who, turning over and over, watched in the sky behind the cross of the window the tingling particles of the white dark, who heard the moth between the two window-sashes, who fancied she heard apples drop in the grass. One arbitrary line only divided this child from the animal: all her senses stood up, wanting to run the night. She swung her legs out of bed and pressed the soles of her feet on the cool floor. She got right up and stepped out of her nightdress and set out to walk the house in her skin. From each room she went into the human order seemed to have lapsed — discovered by sudden light, the chairs and tables seemed set round for a mouse's party on a gigantic scale. She stood for sometime outside the drawing-room door and heard the unliving voices of the Major and Aunt. She looked through the ajar door to the kitchen and saw a picked bone and a teapot upon the table and a maid lumped mute in a man's arms. She attempted the front door, but did not dare to touch the chain: she could not get out of the house. She returned to the schoolroom, drawing her brows together, and straddled the rocking-horse they had not ridden for years. The furious bumping of the rockers woke the canaries under their cover: they set up a wiry springing in their cage. She dismounted, got out the box of chalks and began to tattoo her chest, belly and thighs with stars and snakes, red, yellow and blue. Then, taking the box of chalks with her, she went to her mother's room for a look in the long glass — in front of this she attempted to tattoo her behind. After this she bent right down and squinted, upside down between her legs, at the bedroom — the electric light over the dressing-table poured into the vacantly upturned mirror and on to Emma's left-behind silver things. The anarchy she felt all through the house tonight made her, when she had danced in front of the long glass, climb up to dance on the big bed. The springs bounced her higher and higher; chalk dust flew from her body on to the fleece of the blankets, on to the two cold pillows that she was trampling out of their place. The bed castors lunged, under her springing, over the threadbare pink bridal carpet of Emma's room.

Attacked by the castors the chandelier in the drawing-room tinkled sharply over Aunt Fran's head.

She at once raised her eyes to the ceiling. 'Something has got in,' she said calmly — and, rising, made for the drawing-room door. By reflex, the Major rose to stop her: he sighed and put his weak whiskey down. 'Never mind,' he said, 'Aunt Fran. It's probably nothing. I'll go.'

Whereupon, his Aunt Fran wheeled round on him with her elbows up like a bird's wings. Her wax features sprang into stony prominence. 'It's never me, never me, never me! Whatever *I* see, whatever *I* hear it's "nothing", though the house might fall down. You keep everything back from me. No one speaks the truth to me but the man on the wireless. Always things being said on the telephone, always things being moved about, always Emma off at the end of the house singing, always the children hiding away. I am never told, never told, never told. I get the one answer, "Nothing". I am expected to wait here. No one comes near the drawing-room. I am never allowed to go and see!'

'If that's how you feel,' he said, 'do certainly go.' He thought: it's all right, I locked the house.

So it was Aunt Fran's face, with the forehead lowered, that came by inches round Emma's door. She appeared to present her forehead as a sort of a buffer, obliquely looked from below it, did not speak. Her glance, arriving gradually at its object, took in the child and the whole room. Vivie paused on the bed, transfixed, breathless, her legs apart. Her heart thumped; her ears drummed; her cheeks burned. To break up the canny and comprehensive silence she said loudly: 'I am all over snakes.'

'So this is what . . .' Aunt Fran said. 'So this is what . . .'

'I'll get off this bed, if you don't like.'

'The bed you were born in,' said Aunt Fran.

Vivie did not know what to do; she jumped off the bed saying. 'No one told me not to.'

'Do you not know what is wicked?' said Aunt Fran — but with no more than estranged curiosity. She approached and began to try to straighten the bed, her unused hands making useless passes over the surface, brushing chalk dust deeper into the fleece. All of a sudden, Vivie appeared to feel some majestic effluence from her aunt's person: she lagged round the bed to look at the stooping, set face, at the mouth held in a curve like a dead smile, at the veins in the downcast eyelids and the backs of the hands. Aunt Fran did not hurry her ceremonial fumbling; she seemed to exalt the moment that was so fully hers. She picked a pillow up by its frill and placed it high on the bolster.

'That's Mother's pillow,' said Vivie.

'Did you say your prayers tonight?'

'Oh, *yes.*'

'They didn't defend you. Better say them again. Kneel down and say to Our Lord –'

'In my skin?'

Aunt Fran looked directly at, then away from, Vivie's body, as though for the first time. She drew the eiderdown from the foot of the bed and made a half-blind sweep at Vivie with it, saying: 'Wrap up, wrap up.' 'Oh, they'll come off – my snakes!' said Vivie, backing away.But Aunt Fran, as though the child were on fire, put into motion an extraordinary strength – she rolled, pressed and pounded Vivie up in the eiderdown until only the prisoner's dark eyes, so like her mother's, were left free to move wildly outside the great sausage, of padded taffeta, pink.

Aunt Fran, embracing the sausage firmly, repeated: 'Now say to Our Lord –'

Shutting the door of her own bedroom, Aunt Fran felt her heart beat. The violence of the stranger within her ribs made her sit down on the ottoman – meanwhile, her little clock on the mantelpiece loudly and, it seemed to her, slowly ticked. Her window was shut, but the pressure of night silence made itself felt behind the blind, on the glass.

Round the room, on ledges and brackets, stood the fetishes she travelled through life with. They were mementoes – photos in little warped frames, musty, round straw boxes, china kittens, palm crosses, the three Japanese monkeys, *bambini,* a Lincoln Imp, a merry-thought penwiper, an ivory spinning-wheel from Cologne. From these objects the original virtue had by now almost evaporated.

These gifts' givers, known on her lonely journey, were by now faint as their photographs: she no longer knew, now, where anyone was. All the more, her nature clung to these objects that moved with her slowly towards the dark.

Her room, the room of a person tolerated, by now gave off the familiar smell of herself – the smell of the old. A little book wedged the mirror at the angle she liked. When she was into her ripplecloth dressing-gown she brushed and plaited her hair and took out her teeth. She wound her clock and, with hand still trembling a little, lighted her own candle on the commode, then switched off her nephew's electric light. The room contracted round the crocus of flame as she knelt down slowly beside her bed – but while she said the Lord's Prayer she could not help listening, wondering what kept the Major so long downstairs. She never felt free to pray till she had heard the last door shut, till she could relax her watch on the house. She never could pray until they were *all* prostrate – loaned for at least some hours to innocence, sealed by the darkness over their lids.

Tonight she could not attempt to lift up her heart. She could, however, abase herself, and she abased herself for them all. The evil of the moment down in the drawing-room, the moment when she had cried, 'It is never me!' clung like a smell to her, so closely that she had been eager to get her clothes off, and did not like, even now, to put her hands to her face.

Who shall be their judge? Not I.

The blood of the world is poisoned, feels Aunt Fran, with her forehead over the eiderdown. Not a pure drop comes out at any prick – yes, even the heroes shed black blood. The solitary watcher retreats step by step from his post – who shall stem the black tide coming in? There are no more children: the children are born knowing. The shadow rises up the cathedral tower, up the side of the pure hill. There is not even the past: our memories share with us the infected zone; not a memory does not lead up to this. Each moment is everywhere, it holds the war in its crystal;

there is no elsewhere, no other place. Not a benediction falls on this apart house of the Major; the enemy is within it, creeping about. Each heart here falls to the enemy.

So this is what goes on . . .

Emma flying away – and not saying why, or where. And to wrap the burning child up did not put out the fire. You cannot look at the sky without seeing the shadow, the men destroying each other. What is the matter tonight – is there a battle? This is a threatened night.

Aunt Fran sags on her elbows; her knees push desperately in the woolly rug. She cannot even repent; she is capable of no act; she is undone. She gets up and eats a biscuit, and looks at the little painting of Mont Blanc on the little easel beside her clock. She still does not hear the Major come up to bed.

Queenie understood that the third child, the girl, was dead: she gave back the photograph rather quickly, as though unbearable sadness emanated from it. Justin, however, came down the room and looked at the photograph over Robinson's shoulder – at the rather vulgar, frank, blonde little face. He found it hard to believe that a child of Robinson's should have chosen the part of death. He then went back to the table and picked up, with a jerky effrontery, the photographs of the two little boys. 'Do they never come here?' he said. 'You have plenty of room for them.'

'I daresay they will; I mean to fix up something. Just now they're at Greystones,' Robinson said – he then looked quite openly at the clock.

'With their mother?' Justin said, in a harsh impertinent voice.

'Yes, with my wife.'

'So you keep up the two establishments?'

Even Robinson glanced at Justin with some surprise. 'If you call it that,' he said indifferently. 'I rather landed myself with this place, really – as a matter of fact, when I moved in it looked as though things might work out differently. First I stopped where you are, at the hotel, but I do like to have a place of my own. One feels freer, for one thing.'

'There's a lot in that,' said Justin, with an oblique smile. 'Our local ladies think you keep a Bluebeard's castle up here.'

'What, corpses?' Robinson said, surprised.

'Oh yes, they think you're the devil.'

'Who, me?' replied Robinson, busy replacing photographs on the mantelpiece. 'That's really very funny: I'd no idea. I suppose they may think I've been pretty slack – but I'm no good at teafights, as a matter of fact. But I can't see what else can be eating them. What ought I to do then? Throw a party here? I will if your sister'll come and pour out tea – but I don't think I've really got enough chairs ... I hope,' he added, looking at Queenie, '*she* doesn't think it's not all above board here?'

'You're forgetting again: she misses the talk, poor girl.'

'She doesn't look very worried.'

'I daresay she's seldom been happier. She's built up quite a romance about this house. She has a world to herself – I could envy her.'

Robinson contrived to give the impression that he did not wish to have Queenie discussed – partly because he owned her, he understood her, partly because he wished to discuss nothing: it really was time for his guests to go. Though he was back again in his armchair, regard for time appeared in his attitude. Justin could not fail to connect this with the telephone and the smile that had not completely died. It became clear, staringly clear, that throughout the evening his host had been no more than marking time. This made Justin say 'Yes' (in a loud, pertinacious voice), 'this evening's been quite an event for us. Your house has more than its legend, Robinson; it has really remarkable character. However, all good things –' Stiff with anger, he stood up.

'Must you?' said Robinson, rising, 'I'm so sorry.'

Lighting-up time, fixed by Nature had passed. The deaf

woman, from her place in the window, had been watching lights of cars bend over the hill. Turning with the main road, that had passed the foot of the mountains, each car now drove a shaft of extreme brilliance through the dark below Robinson's pampas grass. Slipping, dropping with a rush past the gate, illuminating the dust on the opposite wall, car after car vanished after its light — there was suddenly quite a gust of them, as though the mountain country, before sleeping, had stood up and shaken them from its folds. The release of movement excited Queenie — that and the beat of light's wings on her face. She turned round very reluctantly as Justin approached and began to make signs to her.

'Why, does Mr. Robinson want us to go?' she said.

'That's the last thing I want!' shouted Robinson.

('She can't hear you.')

'Christ . . .' said Robinson, rattled. He turned the lights on — the three, each with a different face of despair, looked at each other across the exposed room, across the tea tray on the circular table and the superb leather backs of the chairs. 'My brother thinks we've kept you too long.' she said — and as a lady she looked a little shaken, for the first time unsure of herself. Robinson would not for worlds have had this happen; he strode over and took and nursed her elbow, which tensed then relaxed gently inside the muslin sleeve. He saw, outdoors, his window cast on the pampas, saw the whole appearance of shattered night. She looked for reassurance into his face, and he saw the delicate lines in hers.

'And look how late it's got, Mr. Robinson!'

'It's not that,' he said in his naturally low voice, 'But —'

A car pulled up at the gate. Alarmed by the lit window it cut its lights off and could be felt to crouch there, attentive, docile, cautious, waiting to turn in. 'Your friend is arriving,' Justin said.

On that last lap of her drive, the eighteen miles of flat road along the base of the mountains, the last tingling phase of darkness had settled down. Grassy sharpness passed from the mountains' outline, the patches of firs, the gleam of watery ditch. The west sky had gradually drunk its yellow and the ridged heights that towered over her right hand became immobile cataracts, sensed not seen. Animals rising out of the ditches turned to Emma's headlamps green lamp-eyes. She felt the shudder of night, the contracting bodies of things. The quick air sang in her ears; she drove very fast. At the cross-roads above Robinson's town she pulled round in a wide swerve: she saw the lemon lights of the town strung along under the black trees, the pavements and the pale, humble houses below her in a faint, mysterious glare as she slipped down the funnel of hill to Robinson's gate. (The first white gate on the left, you cannot miss it, he'd said.) From the road she peered up the lawn and saw, between pampas tufts, three people upright in his lit room. So she pulled up and switched her lights and her engine off and sat crouching in her crouching car in the dark – night began to creep up her bare legs. Now the glass porch sprang into prominence like a lantern – she saw people stiffly saying goodbye. Down the drive came a man and woman almost in flight; not addressing each other, not looking back – putting the back of a fist to her mouth quickly Emma checked the up-rush of an uncertain laugh. She marked a lag in the steps – turning their heads quickly the man and woman looked with involuntary straightness into the car, while her eyes were glued to their silhouettes. The two turned down to the town and she turned in at the gate.

Farouche, with her tentative little swagger and childish, pleading air of delinquency, Emma came to a halt in Robinson's living-room. He had pulled down the blind. She kept recoiling and blinking and drawing her fingers over her eyes, till Robinson turned off the top light. 'Is that that?' There was only the reading lamp.

She rested her shoulder below his and grappled their enlaced fingers closer together as though trying to draw calmness from him. Standing against him, close up under his height, she held her head up and began to look round the room. 'You're whistling something,' she said, after a moment or two.

'I only mean, take your time.'

'Why, am I nervous?' she said.

'Darling, you're like a bat in out of the night. I told you not to come along too fast.'

'I see now, I came too early,' she said. 'Why didn't you tell me you had a party? Who were they? What were they doing here?'

'Oh, they're just people in this place. He's a bit screwy and she's deaf, but I like them, as a matter of fact.'

'They're mackintoshy sort of people,' she said. 'But I always thought you lived all alone . . . Is there anyone else in the house now?'

'Not a mouse,' said Robinson, without change of expression. 'My housekeeper's gone off for the night.'

'I see,' said Emma. 'Will you give me a drink?'

She sat down where Justin had just been sitting, and, bending forward with a tremulous frown, began to brush ash from the arm of the chair. You could feel the whole of her hesitate. Robinson, without hesitation, came and sat easily on the arm of the chair from which she had brushed the ash. 'It's sometimes funny,' he said, 'when people drop in like that. "My God," I thought when I saw them, "what an evening to choose." ' He slipped his hand down between the brown velvet cushion and Emma's spine, then spread the broad of his hand against the small of her back. Looking kindly down at her closed eyelids he went on: 'However, it all went off all right. Oh, and there's one thing I'd like to tell you – that chap called me a genius.'

'How would he know?' said Emma, opening her eyes.

'We never got that clear. I was rather out of my depth. His sister was deaf . . .' here Robinson paused, bent down and passed his lips absently over Emma's forehead. 'Or did I tell you that?'

'Yes, you told me that . . . Is it true that this house is blue?'

'You'll see tomorrow.'

87

'There'll hardly be time, darling; I shall hardly see this house in the daylight. I must go on to – where I'm supposed to be.'

'At any rate, I'm glad that was all O.K. They're not on the telephone, where you're going?'

'No, it's all right; they're not on the telephone . . . *You'll* have to think of something that went wrong with my car.'

'That will all keep,' said Robinson. 'Here you are.'

'Yes, here I am.' She added: 'The night was lovely,' speaking more sadly than she knew. Yes, here she was, being settled down to as calmly as he might have settled down to a meal. Her naivety as a lover . . . She could not have said, for instance, how much the authoritative male room – the electric clock, the sideboard, the unlit grate, the cold of the leather chairs – put, at every moment when he did not touch her, a gulf between her and him. She turned her head to the window. 'I smell flowers.'

'Yes, I've got three flowerbeds.'

'Darling, for a minute could we go out?'

She moved from his touch and picked up Queenie's tea tray and asked if she could put it somewhere else. Holding the tray (and given countenance by it) she halted in front of the photographs. 'Oh . . .' she said. 'Yes. Why?' 'I wish in a way you hadn't got any children.' 'I don't see why I shouldn't have: you have.'

'Yes, I . . . But Vivie and Di are not so much *like* children –'

'If they're like you,' he said, 'those two will be having a high old time, with the cat away –'

'Oh darling, I'm not the cat.'

In the kitchen (to put the tray down) she looked round: it shone with tiling and chromium and there seemed to be switches in every place. 'What a whole lot of gadgets you have,' she said. 'Look at all those electric . . .' 'Yes I like them.' 'They must cost a lot of money. My kitchen's all over blacklead and smoke and hooks. My cook would hate a kitchen like this.'

'I always forget that you have a cook.' He picked up an

electric torch and they went out. Going along the side of the house, Robinson played a mouse of light on the wall. 'Look, really blue.' But she only looked absently. 'Yes – But have I been wrong to come?' He led her off the gravel on to the lawn, till they reached the edge of a bed of stocks. Then he firmly said: 'That's for you to say, my dear girl.'

'I know it's hardly a question – I hardly know you, do I?'

'We'll be getting to know each other,' said Robinson.

After a minute she let go of his hand and knelt down abruptly beside the flowers: she made movements like scooping the scent up and laving her face in it – he, meanwhile, lighted a cigarette and stood looking down. 'I'm glad you like my garden,' he said. 'You feel like getting fond of the place?'

'You say you forget that I have a cook.'

'Look, sweet, if you can't get that off your mind you'd better get in your car and go straight home . . . But you will.'

'Aunt Fran's so old, too old; it's not nice. And the Major keeps thinking about the war. And the children don't think I am good; I regret that.'

'You have got a nerve,' he said, 'but I love that. You're with me. Aren't you with me? – Come out of that flower-bed.'

They walked to the brow of the lawn; the soft feather-plumes of the pampas rose up a little over her head as she stood by him overlooking the road. She shivered. 'What are those trees?' 'The demesne – I know they burnt down the castle years ago. The demesne's great for couples.' 'What's in there?' 'Nothing, I don't think; just the ruin, a lake . . .'

'I wish –'

'Now, what?'

'I wish we had more time.'

'Yes: we don't want to stay out all night.'

So taught, she smothered the last of her little wishes for

consolation. Her shyness of further words between them became extreme; she was becoming frightened of Robinson's stern, experienced delicacy on the subject of love. Her adventure became the quiet practice with him. The adventure (even, the pilgrimage) died at its root, in the childish part of her mind. When he had headed her off the cytherean terrain — the leaf-drowned castle ruin, the lake — she thought for a minute he had broken her heart, and she knew now he had broken her fairytale. He seemed content — having lit a new cigarette — to wait about in his garden for a few minutes longer: not poetry but a sort of tactile wisdom came from the firmness, lawn, under their feet. The white gateposts, the boles of beeches above the dust-whitened wall were just seen in reflected light from the town. There was no moon, but dry, tense, translucent darkness: no dew fell.

Justin went with his sister to her door in the square. Quickly, and in their necessary silence, they crossed the grass under the limes. Here a dark window reflected one of the few lamps, there a shadow crossed a lit blind, and voices of people moving under the trees made a reverberation in the box of the square. Queenie let herself in; Justin heard the heavy front door drag shut slowly across the mat. She had not expected him to come in, and he did not know if she shared his feeling of dissonance, or if she recoiled from shock, or if she were shocked at all. Quitting the square at once, he took the direct way to his hotel in the main street. He went in at the side door, past the bar in which he so often encountered Robinson.

In his small, harsh room he looked first at his bed. He looked, as though out of a pit of sickness, at his stack of books on the mantelpiece. He writhed his head round sharply, threw off his coat and began to unknot his tie. Meanwhile he beat round, in the hot light, for some crack of outlet from his constriction. It was at his dressing-table, for he had no other, that he began and ended his letter to Robinson: the mirror screwed to the dressing-table constituted a witness to this task – whenever his look charged up it met his own reared head, the flush heightening on the bridge of the nose and forehead, the neck from which, as though for an execution, the collar had been taken away.

My dear Robinson: Our departure from your house (Bellevue, I think?) tonight was so awkwardly late, and at the last so hurried, that I had inadequate time in which to thank you for your hospitality to my sister and to myself. That we exacted this hospitality does not make its merit, on your part, less. Given the inconvenience we so clearly caused you, your forbearance with us was past praise. So much so that (as you may be glad to hear) my sister does not appear to realise how very greatly we were *de trop*. In my own case – which is just – the same cannot be said. I am conscious that, in spite of her disability, she did at least prove a less wearisome guest than I.

My speculations and queries must, to your mind, equally seem absurd. This evening's fiasco has been definitive: I think it better our acquaintance should close. You will find it in line with my usual awkwardness that I should choose to state this decision of mine at all. Your indifference to the matter I cannot doubt. My own lack of indifference must make its last weak exhibition in this letter – in which, if you have fine enough nostrils (which I doubt), every sentence will almost certainly stink. In attempting to know you I have attempted to enter, and to comport myself in, what might be called an area under your jurisdiction. If my inefficacies appeared to you ludicrous, my curiosities (as in one special instance tonight) appeared more-revolting. I could gauge (even before the postscript outside your gate) how profoundly I had offended you. Had we either of us been gentlemen, the incident might have passed off with less harm.

My attempts to know you I have disposed of already. My wish that you should know me has been, from the first, ill found. You showed yourself party to it in no sense, and the trick I played on myself I need not discuss. I acted and spoke (with regard to you) upon assumptions you were not prepared to warrant. You cannot fail to misunderstand what I mean when I say that a year ago this might not have happened to me. But — the assumptions on which I acted, Robinson, are becoming more general in a driven world than you yet (or may ever) know. The extremity to which we are each driven must be the warrant for what we do and say.

My extraordinary divagation towards you might be said to be, I suppose, an accident of this summer. But there are no accidents. I have the fine (yes) fine mind's love of the fine plume, and I meet no fine plumes down my own narrow street. Also, in this place (birthplace) you interposed your solidity between me and what might have been the full effects of an exacerbating return. In fact, you had come to constitute for me a very genuine holiday. As things are, my five remaining days here will have to be seen out. I shall hope not to meet you, but must fear much of the trap-like size of this town. (You need not, as I mean to, avoid the hotel bar.) Should I, however, fail to avoid you, I shall again, I suppose, have to owe much, owe any face I keep, to your never-failing imperviousness. Understand that it will be against my wish that I re-open this one-sided account.

I wish you good night. Delicacy does not deter me from adding that I feel my good wish to be superfluous. I imagine that, incapable of being haunted, you are incapable of being added to. Tomorrow (I understand) you will feel fine, but you will not know any more about love. If the being outside your gate came with a question, it is possible that she should have come to me. If I had even seen her she might not go on rending my heart. As it is, as you are, I perhaps denounce you as much on her behalf as my own. Not trying to understand, you at least cannot misunderstand the mood and hour in which I write. As regards my sister, please do not discontinue what has been your even kindness to her: she might be perplexed. She has nothing to fear, I think.

Accept, my dear Robinson (without irony) my kind regards,

J. C.

Justin, trembling, smote a stamp on this letter. Going down as he was, in the hall he unhooked his mackintosh and put it over his shirt. It was well past midnight; the street, empty, lay in dusty reaches under the few lamps. Between the shutters his step raised an echo; the cold of the mountains had come down; two cats in his path unclinched and shot off into the dark. On his way to the letterbox he was walking towards Bellevue; on his way back he still heard the drunken woman sobbing against the telegraph pole. The box would not be cleared till tomorrow noon.

Queenie forgot Justin till next day. The house in which her rooms were was so familiar that she went upstairs without a pause in the dark. Crossing her sitting-room she smelled oil from the cooker behind the screen: she went through an arch to the cubicle where she slept. She was happy. Inside her sphere of silence that not a word clouded, the spectacle of the evening at Bellevue reigned. Contemplative, wishless, almost without an 'I', she unhooked her muslin dress at the wrists and waist, stepped from the dress and began to take down her hair. Still in the dark, with a dreaming sureness of habit, she dropped hairpins into the heart-shaped tray.

This was the night she knew she would find again. It had stayed living under a film of time. On just such a summer night, once only, she had walked with a lover in the demesne. His hand, like Robinson's, had been on her elbow, but she had guided him, not he her, because she had better eyes in the dark. They had gone down walks already deadened with moss, under the weight of July trees; they had felt the then fresh aghast ruin totter above them; there was a moonless sky. Beside the lake they sat down, and while her hand brushed the ferns in the cracks of the stone seat emanations of kindness passed from him to her. The subtle deaf girl had made the transposition of this nothing or everything into an everything – the delicate deaf girl that the man could not speak to and was afraid to touch. She who, then so deeply contented, kept in her senses each frond and breath of that night, never saw him again and had soon forgotten his face. That had been twenty years ago, till tonight when it was now, Tonight it was Robinson who, guided by Queenie down leaf tunnels, took the place on the stone seat by the lake.

The rusted gates of the castle were at the end of the square, Queenie, in her bed facing the window, lay with her face turned sideways, smiling, one hand lightly against her cheek.

The Happy Autumn Fields

The family walking party, though it comprised so many, did not deploy or straggle over the stubble but kept in a procession of threes and twos. Papa, who carried his Alpine stick, led, flanked by Constance and little Arthur. Robert and Cousin Theodore, locked in studious talk, had Emily attached but not quite abreast. Next came Digby and Lucius, taking, to left and right, imaginary aim at rooks. Henrietta and Sarah brought up the rear.

It was Sarah who saw the others ahead on the blond stubble, who knew them, knew what they were to each other, knew their names and knew her own. It was she who felt the stubble under her feet, and who heard it give beneath the tread of the others a continuous different more distant soft stiff scrunch. The field and all these outlying fields in view knew as Sarah knew that they were Papa's. The harvest had been good and was now in: he was satisfied – for this afternoon he had made the instinctive choice of his most womanly daughter, most nearly infant son. Arthur, whose hand Papa was holding, took an anxious hop, a skip and a jump to every stride of the great man's. As for Constance – Sarah could often see the flash of her hat feather as she turned her head, the curve of her close bodice as she turned her torso. Constance gave Papa her attention but not her thoughts, for she had already been sought in marriage.

The landowner's daughters, from Constance down, walked with their beetle-green, mole or maroon skirts gathered up and carried clear of the ground, but for Henrietta, who was still ankle-free. They walked inside a continuous stuffy sound, but left silence behind them. Behind them, rooks that had risen and circled, sun striking blue from their blue-black wings, planed one by one to the earth and settled to peck again. Papa and the boys were dark-clad as the rooks but with no sheen, but for their white collars.

It was Sarah who located the thoughts of Constance, knew what a twisting prisoner was Arthur's hand, felt to the depths of Emily's pique at Cousin Theodore's inattention, rejoiced with Digby and Lucius at the imaginary fall of so many rooks. She fell back, however, as from a rocky range, from the converse of Robert and Cousin Theodore. Most she knew that she swam with love at the nearness of Henrietta's young and alert face and eyes which shone with the sky and queried the afternoon.

She recognised the colour of valediction, tasted sweet sadness, while from the cottage inside the screen of trees wood smoke rose melting pungent and blue. This was the eve of the brothers' return to school. It was like a Sunday; Papa had kept the late afternoon free; all (all but one) encircling Robert, Digby and Lucius, they walked the estate the brothers would not see again for so long. Robert, it could be felt, was not unwilling to return to his books; next year he would go to college like Theodore; to all this they saw he was not the heir. But in Digby and Lucius aiming and popping hid a bodily grief, the repugnance of victims, though these two were further from being heirs than Robert.

Sarah said to Henrietta: 'To think they will not be here tomorrow!'

'*Is* that what you are thinking about?' Henrietta asked, with her subtle taste for the truth.

'More, I was thinking that you and I will be back again by one another at table. . . .'

'You know we are always sad when the boys are going, but we are never sad when the boys have gone.' The sweet reciprocal guilty smile that started on Henrietta's lips finished on those of Sarah. 'Also,' the young sister said, 'we know this is only something happening again. It happened last year, and it will happen next. But oh how should I feel, and how should you feel, if it were something that had not happened before?'

'For instance, when Constance goes to be married?'

'Oh, I don't mean *Constance!*' said Henrietta.

'So long,' said Sarah, considering, 'as whatever it is, it happens to both of us?' She must never have to wake in the early morning except to the birdlike stirrings of Henrietta, or have her cheek brushed in the dark by the frill of another pillow in whose hollow did not repose Henrietta's cheek. Rather than they should cease to lie in the same bed she prayed they might lie in the same grave. 'You and I will stay as we are,' she said, 'then nothing can touch one without touching the other.'

'So you say; so I hear you say!' exclaimed Henrietta, who then, lips apart, sent Sarah her most tormenting look. 'But I cannot forget that you chose to be born without me; that you would not wait – ' But here she broke off, laughed outright and said: 'Oh, *see!*'

Ahead of them there had been a dislocation. Emily took advantage of having gained the ridge to kneel down to tie her bootlace so abruptly that Digby all but fell over her, with an exclamation. Cousin Theodore had been civil enough to pause beside Emily, but Robert, lost to all but what he was saying, strode on, head down, only just not colliding into Papa and Constance, who had turned to look back. Papa, astounded, let go of Arthur's hand, whereupon Arthur fell flat on the stubble.

'Dear me,' said the affronted Constance to Robert.

Papa said: 'What is the matter there? May I ask, Robert, where you are going, sir? Digby, remember that is your sister Emily.'

'Cousin Emily is in trouble,' said Cousin Theodore.

Poor Emily, telescoped in her skirts and by now scarlet under her hatbrim, said in a muffled voice: 'It is just my bootlace, Papa.'

'Your bootlace, Emily?'

'I was just tying it.'

'Then you had better tie it. – Am I to think,' said Papa, looking round them all, 'that you must all go down like a pack of ninepins because Emily has occasion to stoop?'

At this Henrietta uttered a little whoop, flung her arms round Sarah, buried her face in her sister and fairly suffered with laughter. She could contain this no longer; she shook all over. Papa who found Henrietta so hopelessly out of order that he took no notice of her except at table, took no notice, simply giving the signal for the others to collect themselves and move on. Cousin Theodore, helping Emily to her feet, could be seen to see how her heightened colour became her, but she dispensed with his hand chillily, looked elsewhere, touched the brooch at her throat and said: 'Thank you, I have not sustained an accident.' Digby apologised to Emily, Robert to Papa and Constance. Constance righted Arthur, flicking his breeches over with her handkerchief. All fell into their different steps and resumed their way.

Sarah, with no idea how to console laughter, coaxed, 'Come, come, come,' into Henrietta's ear. Between the girls and the others the distance widened; it began to seem that they would be left alone.

'And why not?' said Henrietta, lifting her head in answer to Sarah's thought.

They looked around them with the same eyes. The shorn uplands seemed to float on the distance, which extended dazzling to tiny blue glassy hills. There was no end to the afternoon, whose light went on ripening now they had scythed the corn. Light filled the silence which, now Papa and the others were out of hearing, was complete. Only screens of trees intersected and knolls made islands in the vast fields. The mansion and the home farm had sunk for ever below them in the expanse of woods, so that hardly a ripple showed where the girls dwelled.

The shadow of the same rook circling passed over Sarah then over Henrietta, who in their turn cast one shadow across the stubble. 'But, Henrietta, we cannot stay here for ever.'

Henrietta immediately turned her eyes to the only lonely plume of smoke, from the cottage. 'Then let us go and visit the poor old man. He is dying and the others are happy. One day we shall pass and see no more smoke: then soon his roof will fall in, and we shall always be sorry we did not go today.'

'But he no longer remembers us.'

'All the same, he will feel us there in the door.'

'But can we forget this is Robert's and Digby's and Lucius's goodbye walk? It would be heartless of both of us to neglect them.'

'Then how heartless Fitzgeorge is!' smiled Henrietta.

'Fitzgeorge is himself, the eldest and in the Army. Fitzgeorge I'm afraid is not an excuse for us.'

A resigned sigh, or perhaps the pretence of one, heaved up Henrietta's still narrow bosom. To delay matters for just a moment more she shaded her eyes with one hand, to search the distance like a sailor looking for a sail. She gazed with hope and zeal in every direction but that in which she and Sarah were bound to go. Then – 'Oh, but Sarah, here *they* are, coming – they are!' she cried. She brought out her handkerchief and began to fly it, drawing it to and fro through the windless air.

In the glass of the distance, two horsemen came into view, cantering on a grass track between the fields. When the track dropped into a hollow they dropped with it, but by now the drumming of hoofs was heard. The reverberation filled the land, the silence and Sarah's being; not watching for the riders to reappear she instead fixed her eyes on her sister's handkerchief which, let hang limp while its owner intently waited, showed a bitten corner as well as a damson stain. Again it became a flag, in furious motion. – 'Wave too, Sarah, wave too! Make your bracelet flash!'

'They must have seen us if they will ever see us,' said Sarah, standing still as a stone.

Henrietta's waving at once ceased. Facing her sister she

crunched up her handkerchief, as though to stop it acting a lie. 'I can see you are shy,' she said in a dead voice. 'So shy you won't even wave to *Fitzgeorge*?'

Her way of not speaking the *other* name had a hundred meanings; she drove them all in by the way she did not look at Sarah's face. The impulsive breath she had caught stole silently out again, while her eyes – till now at their brightest, their most speaking – dulled with uncomprehending solitary alarm. The ordeal of awaiting Eugene's approach thus became for Sarah, from moment to moment, torture.

Fitzgeorge, Papa's heir, and his friend Eugene, the young neighbouring squire, struck off the track and rode up at a trot with their hats doffed. Sun striking low turned Fitzgeorge's flesh to coral and made Eugene blink his dark eyes. The young men reined in; the girls looked up the horses. 'And my father, Constance, the others?' Fitzgeorge demanded, as though the stubble had swallowed them.

'Ahead, on the way to the quarry, the other side of the hill.'

'We heard you were all walking together,' Fitzgeorge said, seeming dissatisfied.

'We are following.'

'What, alone?' said Eugene, speaking for the first time.

'Forlorn!' glittered Henrietta, raising two mocking hands.

Fitzgeorge considered, said 'Good' severely, and signified to Eugene that they would ride on. But too late: Eugene had dismounted. Fitzgeorge saw, shrugged and flicked his horse to a trot; but Eugene led his slowly between the sisters. Or rather, Sarah walked on his left hand, the horse on his right and Henrietta the other side of the horse. Henrietta, acting like somebody quite alone, looked up at the sky, idly holding one of the empty stirrups. Sarah, however, looked at the ground, with Eugene inclined as though to speak but not speaking. Enfolded, dizzied, blinded as though inside a wave, she could feel his features carved in brightness above her. Alongside the slender stepping of his horse, Eugene matched his naturally long free step to hers. His elbow was through the reins; with his fingers he brushed back the lock that his bending to her had sent falling over his forehead. She recorded the sublime act and knew what smile shaped his lips. So each without looking trembled before an image, while slow colour burned up the curves of her cheeks. The consummation would be when their eyes met.

At the other side of the horse, Henrietta began to sing. At once her pain, like a scientific ray, passed through the horse and Eugene to penetrate Sarah's heart.

We surmount the skyline: the family come into our view, we into theirs. They are halted, waiting, on the decline to the quarry. The handsome statuefied group in strong yellow sunshine, aligned by Papa and crowned by Fitzgeorge, turn their judging eyes on the laggards, waiting to close their ranks round Henrietta and Sarah and Eugene. One more moment and it will be too late; no further communication will be possible. Stop oh stop Henrietta's heartbreaking singing! Embrace her close again! Speak the only possible word! Say – oh, say what? Oh, the word is lost!

'*Henrietta . . .*'
A shock of striking pain in the knuckles of the outflung hand – Sarah's? The eyes, opening, saw that the hand had struck, not been struck: there was a corner of a table. Dust, whitish and gritty, lay on the top of the table and on the telephone. Dull but piercing white light filled the room and what was left of the ceiling; her first thought was that it must have snowed. If so, it was winter now.

Through the calico stretched and tacked over the window came the sound of a piano: someone was playing Tchaikowsky badly in a room without windows or doors. From somewhere else in the hollowness came a cascade of hammering. Close up, a voice: 'oh, *awake*, Mary?' It came from the other side of the open door, which jutted out between herself and the speaker – he on the threshold, she

101

lying on the uncovered mattress of a bed. The speaker added: 'I had been going away.'

Summoning words from somewhere she said: 'Why? I didn't know you were here.'

'Evidently — Say, who is "Henrietta"?'

Despairing tears filled her eyes. She drew back her hurt hand, began to suck at the knuckle and whimpered, 'I've hurt myself.'

A man she knew to be 'Travis', but failed to focus, came round the door saying: 'Really I don't wonder.' Sitting down on the edge of the mattress he drew her hand away from her lips and held it: the act, in itself gentle, was accompanied by an almost hostile stare of concern. 'Do listen, Mary,' he said. 'While you've slept I've been all over the house again, and I'm less than ever satisfied that it's safe. In your normal senses you'd never attempt to stay here. There've been alerts, and more than alerts, all day; one more bang anywhere near, which may happen at any moment, could bring the rest of this down. You keep telling me that you have things to see to — but do you know what chaos the rooms are in? Till they've gone ahead with more clearing, where can you hope to start? And if there *were* anything you could do, you couldn't do it. Your own nerves know that, if you don't: it was almost frightening, when I looked in just now, to see the way you were sleeping — you've shut up shop.'

She lay staring over his shoulder at the calico window. He went on: 'You don't like it here. Your self doesn't like it. Your will keeps driving your self, but it can't be driven the whole way — it makes its own get-out: sleep. Well, I want you to sleep as much as you (really) do. But *not* here. So I've taken a room for you in a hotel; I'm going now for a taxi; you can practically make the move without waking up.'

'No, I can't get into a taxi without waking.'

'Do you realise you're the last soul left in the terrace?'

'Then who is that playing the piano?'

'Oh, one of the furniture-movers in Number Six. I

didn't count the jaquerie; of course *they're* in possession — unsupervised, teeming, having a high old time. While I looked in on you in here ten minutes ago they were smashing out that conservatory at the other end. Glass being done in in cold blood — it was brutalising. You never batted an eyelid; in fact, I thought you smiled.' He listened. 'Yes, the piano — they are highbrow all right. You know there's a workman downstairs lying on your blue sofa looking for pictures in one of your French books?'

'No,' she said, 'I've no idea who is there.'

'Obviously. With the lock blown off your front door anyone who likes can get in and out.'

'Including you.'

'Yes. I've had a word with a chap about getting that lock back before tonight. As for you, you don't know what is happening.'

'I did,' she said, locking her fingers before her eyes.

The unreality of this room and of Travis's presence preyed on her as figments of dreams that one knows to be dreams can do. This environment's being in semi-ruin struck her less than its being some sort of device or trap; and she rejoiced, if anything, in its decrepitude. As for Travis, he had his own part in the conspiracy to keep her from the beloved two. She felt he began to feel he was now unmeaning. She was struggling not to contemn him, scorn him for his ignorance of Henrietta, Eugene, her loss. His possessive angry fondness was part, of course, of the story of him and Mary, which like a book once read she remembered clearly but with indifference. Frantic at being delayed here, while the moment awaited her in the cornfield, she all but afforded a smile at the grotesquerie of being saddled with Mary's body and lover. Rearing up her head from the bare pillow, she looked, as far as the crossed feet, along the form inside which she found herself trapped: the irrelevant body of Mary, weighted down to the bed, wore a short black modern dress, flaked with plaster. The toes of the black suède shoes by their sickly whiteness showed Mary must have climbed over fallen ceilings; dirt engraved the fate lines in Mary's palms.

This inspired her to say: 'But I've made a start; I've been pulling out things of value or things I want.'

For answer Travis turned to look down, expressively, at some object out of her sight, on the floor close by the bed. '*I* see,' he said, 'a musty old leather box gaping open with God knows what — junk, illegible letters, diaries, yellow photographs, chiefly plaster and dust. Of all things, Mary! — after a missing will?'

'Everything one unburies seems the same age.'

'Then what are these, where do they come from — family stuff?'

'No idea,' she yawned into Mary's hand. 'They may not even be mine. Having a house like this that had empty rooms must have made me store more than I knew, for years. I came on these, so I wondered. Look if you like.'

He bent and began to go through the box — it seemed to her, not unsuspiciously. While he blew grit off packets and fumbled with tapes she lay staring at the exposed laths of the ceiling, calculating. She then said: 'Sorry if I've been cranky, about the hotel and all. Go away just for two hours, then come back with a taxi, and I'll go quiet. Will that do?'

'Fine — except why not now?'

'*Travis* . . . .'

'Sorry. It shall be as you say. . . . You've got some good morbid stuff in this box, Mary — so far as I can see at a glance. The photographs seem more your sort of thing. Comic but lyrical. All of one set of people — a beard, a gun and a pot hat, a schoolboy with a moustache, a phaeton drawn up in front of mansion, a group on steps, a *carte de visite* of two young ladies hand-in-hand in front of a painted field — '

'*Give that to me!*'

She instinctively tried and failed, to unbutton the bosom of Mary's dress: it offered no hospitality to the photograph. So she could only fling herself over on the mattress, away from Travis, covering the two faces with her body. Racked by that oblique look of Henrietta's she recorded, too, a sort of personal shock at having seen Sarah for the first time.

Travis's hand came over her, and she shuddered. Wounded, he said: 'Mary . . .'.

'Can't you leave *me* alone?'

She did not move or look till he had gone out saying: 'Then, in two hours.' She did not therefore see him pick up the dangerous box, which he took away under his arm, out of her reach.

They were back. Now the sun was setting behind the trees, but its rays passed dazzling between the branches into the beautiful warm red room. The tips of the ferns in the jardinière curled gold, and Sarah, standing by the jardinière, pinched at a leaf of scented geranium. The carpet had a great centre wreath of pomegranates, on which no tables or chairs stood, and its whole circle was between herself and the others.

No fire was lit yet, but where they were grouped was a hearth. Henrietta sat on a low stool, resting her elbow above her head on the arm of Mamma's chair, looking away intently as though into a fire, idle. Mamma embroidered, her needle slowed down by her thoughts; the length of tatting with roses she had already done overflowed stiffly over her supple skirts. Stretched on the rug at Mamma's feet, Arthur looked through an album of Swiss views, not liking them but vowed to be very quiet. Sarah, from where she stood, saw fuming cataracts and null eternal snows as poor Arthur kept turning over the pages, which had tissue paper between.

Against the white marble mantelpiece stood Eugene. The dark red shadows gathering in the drawing-room as the trees drowned more and more of the sun would reach him last, perhaps never: it seemed to Sarah that a lamp was lighted behind his face. He was the only gentleman with the ladies: Fitzgeorge had gone to the stables, Papa to give an order; Cousin Theodore was consulting a dictionary; in the gunroom Robert, Lucius and Digby went through the sad rites, putting away their guns. All this was known to go on but none of it could be heard.

This particular hour of subtle light – not to be fixed by the clock, for it was early in winter and late in summer and in spring and autumn now, about Arthur's bedtime – had always, for Sarah, been Henrietta's. To be with her indoors or out, upstairs or down, was to share the same crepitation. Her spirit ran on past yours with a laughing shiver into an element of its own. Leaves and branches and mirrors in empty rooms became animate. The sisters rustled and scampered and concealed themselves where nobody else was in play that was full of fear, fear that was full of play. Till, by dint of making each other's hearts beat violently, Henrietta so wholly and Sarah so nearly lost all human reason that Mamma had been known to look at them searchingly as she sat instated for evening among the calm amber lamps.

But now Henrietta had locked the hour inside her breast. By spending it seated beside Mamma, in young imitation of Constance the Society daughter, she disclaimed for ever anything else. It had always been she who with one fierce act destroyed any toy that might be outgrown. She sat with straight back, poising her cheek remotely against her finger. Only by never looking at Sarah did she admit their eternal loss.

Eugene, not long returned from a foreign tour, spoke of travel, addressing himself to Mamma, who thought but did not speak of her wedding journey. But every now and then she had to ask Henrietta to pass the scissors or tray of carded wools, and Eugene seized every such moment to look at Sarah. Into eyes always brilliant with melancholy he dared begin to allow no other expression. But this in itself declared the conspiracy of still undeclared love. For her part she looked at him as though he, transfigured by the strange light, were indeed a picture, a picture who could not see her. The wallpaper now flamed scarlet behind his shoulder. Mamma, Henrietta, even unknowing Arthur were in no hurry to raise their heads.

Henrietta said: 'If I were a man I should take my bride to Italy.'

'There are mules in Switzerland,' said Arthur.

'Sarah,' said Mamma, who turned in her chair mildly, 'where are you, my love; do you never mean to sit down?'

'To Naples,' said Henrietta.

'Are you not thinking of Venice?' said Eugene.

'No,' returned Henrietta, 'why should I be? I should like to climb the volcano. But then I am not a man, and am still less likely ever to be a bride.'

'Arthur . . .' Mamma said.

'Mamma?'

'Look at the clock.'

Arthur sighed politely, got up and replaced the album on the circular table, balanced upon the rest. He offered his hand to Eugene, his cheek to Henrietta and to Mamma; then he started towards Sarah, who came to meet him. 'Tell me, Arthur,' she said, embracing him, 'what did you do today?'

Arthur only stared with his button blue eyes. 'You were there too; we went for a walk in the cornfield, with Fitzgeorge on his horse, and I fell down.' He pulled out of her arms and said: 'I must go back to my beetle.' He had difficulty, as always, in turning the handle of the mahogany door. Mamma waited till he had left the room, then said: 'Arthur is quite a man now; he no longer comes running to me when he has hurt himself. Why, I did not even know he had fallen down. Before we know, he will be going away to school too.' She sighed and lifted her eyes to Eugene. 'Tomorrow is to be a sad day.'

Eugene with a gesture signified his own sorrow. The sentiments of Mamma could have been uttered only here in the drawing-room, which for all its size and formality was lyrical and almost exotic. There was a look like velvet in darker parts of the air; sombre window draperies let out gushes of lace; the music on the pianoforte bore tender titles, and the harp though unplayed gleamed in a corner, beyond sofas, whatnots, armchairs, occasional tables that all stood on tottering little feet. At any moment a tinkle might have been struck from the lustres' drops of the brighter day, a vibration from the musical instruments, or a quiver from the fringes and ferns. But the towering vases upon the consoles, the albums piled on the tables, the shells and figurines on the flights of brackets, all had, like the alabaster Leaning Tower of Pisa, an equilibrium of their own. Nothing would fall or change. And everything in the drawing-room was muted, weighted, pivoted by Mamma. When she added: 'We shall not feel quite the same', it was to be understood that she would not have spoken thus from her place at the opposite end of Papa's table.

'Sarah,' said Henrietta curiously, 'what made you ask Arthur what he had been doing? Surely you have not forgotten today?'

The sisters were seldom known to address or question one another in public; it was taken that they knew each other's minds. Mamma, though untroubled, looked from one to the other. Henrietta continued: 'No day, least of all today, is like any other – Surely that must be true?' she said to Eugene. 'You will never forget my waving my handkerchief?'

Before Eugene had composed an answer, she turned to Sarah: 'Or *you*, them riding across the fields?'

Eugene also slowly turned his eyes on Sarah, as though awaiting with something like dread her answer to the question he had not asked. She drew a light little gold chair into the middle of the wreath of the carpet, where no one ever sat, and sat down. She said: 'But since then I think I have been asleep.'

'Charles the First walked and talked half an hour after his head was cut off,' said Henrietta mockingly. Sarah in anguish pressed the palms of her hands together upon a shred of geranium leaf.

'How else,' she said, 'could I have had such a bad

dream?'

'That must be the explanation!' said Henrietta.

'A trifle fanciful,' said Mamma.

However rash it might be to speak at all, Sarah wished she knew how to speak more clearly. The obscurity and loneliness of her trouble was not to be borne. How could she put into words the feeling of dislocation, the formless dread that had been with her since she found herself in the drawing-room? The source of both had been what she must call her dream. How could she tell the others with what vehemence she tried to attach her being to each second, not because each was singular in itself, each a drop condensed from the mist of love in the room, but because she apprehended that the seconds were numbered? Her hope was that the others at least half knew. Were Henrietta and Eugene able to understand how completely, how nearly for ever, she had been swept from them, would they not without fail each grasp one of her hands? — She went so far as to throw her hands out, as though alarmed by a wasp. The shred of geranium fell to the carpet.

Mamma, tracing this behaviour of Sarah's to only one cause, could not but think reproachfully of Eugene. Delightful as his conversation had been, he would have done better had he paid this call with the object of inter- viewing Papa. Turning to Henrietta she asked her to ring for the lamps, as the sun had set.

Eugene, no longer where he had stood, was able to make no gesture towards the bell-rope. His dark head was under the tide of dusk; for, down on one knee on the edge of the wreath, he was feeling over the carpet for what had fallen from Sarah's hand. In the inevitable silence rooks on the return from the fields could be heard streaming over the house; their sound filled the sky and even the room, and it appeared so useless to ring the bell that Henrietta stayed quivering by Mamma's chair. Eugene rose, brought out his fine white handkerchief and, while they watched, enfolded carefully in it what he had just found, then returning the handkerchief to his breast pocket. This was done so deep in the reverie that accompanies any final act that Mamma instinctively murmured to Henrietta: 'But you will be my child when Arthur has gone.'

The door opened for Constance to appear on the threshold. Behind her queenly figure globes approached, swimming in their own light: these were the lamps for which Henrietta had not rung, but these first were put on the hall tables. 'Why, Mamma,' exclaimed Constance, 'I cannot see who is with you!'

'Eugene is with us,' said Henrietta, 'but on the point of asking if he may send for his horse.'

'Indeed?' said Constance to Eugene. 'Fitzgeorge has been asking for you, but I cannot tell where he is now.'

The figures of Emily, Lucius and Cousin Theodore criss-crossed the lamplight there in the hall, to mass behind Constance's in the drawing-room door. Emily, over her sister's shoulder, said: 'Mamma, Lucius wishes to ask you whether for once he may take his guitar to school.' — 'One objection, however,' said Cousin Theodore, 'is that Lucius's trunk is already locked and strapped.' 'Since Robert is taking his box of inks,' said Lucius, 'I do not see why I should not take my guitar.' — 'But Robert,' said Constance, 'will soon be going to college.'

Lucius squeezed past the others into the drawing-room in order to look anxiously at Mamma, who said: 'You have thought of this late; we must go and see.' The others parted to let Mamma, followed by Lucius, out. Then Constance, Emily and Cousin Theodore deployed and sat down in different parts of the drawing-room, to await the lamps.

'I am glad the rooks have done passing over,' said Emily, 'they make me nervous.' — 'Why?' yawned Constance haughtily, 'what do you think could happen?' Robert and Digby silently came in.

Eugene said to Sarah: 'I shall be back tomorrow.'

'But, oh — ' she began. She turned to cry: 'Henrietta!'

'Why, what is the matter?' said Henrietta, unseen at the

back of the gold chair. 'What could be sooner than tomorrow?'

'But something terrible may be going to happen.'

'There cannot fail to be tomorrow,' said Eugene grave-ly.

'*I* will see that there is tomorrow,' said Henrietta.

'You will never let me out of your sight?'

Eugene, addressing himself to Henrietta, said: 'Yes, promise her what she asks.'

Henrietta cried: 'She *is* never out of my sight. Who are you to ask me that, you Eugene? Whatever tries to come between me and Sarah becomes nothing. Yes, come tomorrow, come sooner, come — when you like, but no one will ever be quite alone with Sarah. You do not even know what you are trying to do. It is *you* who are making something terrible happen. — Sarah, tell him that that is true! Sarah — '

The others, in the dark on the chairs and sofas, could be felt to turn their judging eyes upon Sarah, who, as once before, could not speak —

— The house rocked: simultaneously the calico window split and more ceiling fell, though not on the bed, The enormous dull sound of the explosion died, leaving a minor trickle of dissolution still to be heard in parts of the house. Until the choking stinging plaster dust had had time to settle, she lay with lips pressed close, nostrils not breathing and eyes shut. Remembering the box, Mary wondered if it had been again buried. No, she found, looking over the edge of the bed: that had been unable to happen because the box was missing. Travis, who must have taken it, would when he came back no doubt explain why. She looked at her watch, which had stopped, which was not surprising; she did not remember winding it for the last two days, but then she could not remember much. Through the torn window appeared the timelessness of an impermeably clouded late summer afternoon.

There being nothing left, she wished he would come to

take her to the hotel. The one way back to the fields was barred by Mary's surviving the fall of ceiling. Sarah was right in doubting that there would be tomorrow: Eugene, Henrietta were lost in time to the woman weeping there on the bed, no longer reckoning who she was.

At last she heard the taxi, then Travis hurrying up the littered stairs. 'Mary, you're all right, Mary — *another*?' Such a helpless white face came round the door that she could only hold out her arms and say: 'Yes, but where have *you* been?'

'You said two hours. But I wish — '

'I have missed you.'

'Have you? Do you know you are crying?'

'Yes. How are we to live without natures? We only know inconvenience now, not sorrow. Everything pulverises so easily because it is rot-dry; one can only wonder that it makes so much noise. The source, the sap must have dried up, or the pulse must have stopped, before you and I were conceived. So much flowed through people; so little flows through us. All we can do is imitate love or sorrow. — Why did you take away my box?'

He only said: 'It is in my office.'

She continued: 'What has happened is cruel: I am left with a fragment torn out of a day, a day I don't even know where or when; and now how am I to help laying that like a pattern against the poor stuff of everything else? — Alternatively, I am a person drained by a dream. I cannot forget the climate of those hours. Or life at that pitch, eventful — not happy, no, but strung like a harp. I have had a sister called Henrietta.'

'And I have been looking inside your box. What else can you expect? — I have had to write off this day, from the work point of view, thanks to you. So could I sit and do nothing for the last two hours? I just glanced through this and that — still, I know the family.'

'You said it was morbid stuff.'

'Did I? I still say it gives off something.'

She said: 'And then there was Eugene.'

'Probably. I don't think I came on much of his except some notes he must have made for Fitzgeorge from some book on scientific farming. Well, there it is: I have sorted everything out and put it back again, all but a lock of hair that tumbled out of a letter I could not trace. So I've got the hair in my pocket.'

'What colour is it?'

'Ash-brown. Of course, it is a bit – desiccated. Do you want it?'

'No,' she said with a shudder. 'Really, Travis, what revenges you take!'

'I didn't look at it that way,' he said puzzled.

'Is the taxi waiting?' Mary got off the bed and, picking her way across the room, began to look about for things she ought to take with her, now and then stopping to brush her dress. She took the mirror out of her bag to see how dirty her face was. 'Travis – ' she said suddenly.

'Mary?'

'Only, I – '

'That's all right. Don't let us imitate anything just at present.'

In the taxi, looking out of the window, she said: 'I suppose, then, that I am descended from Sarah?'

'No,' he said, 'that would be impossible. There must be some reason why you should have those papers, but that is not the one. From all negative evidence Sarah, like Henrietta, remained unmarried. I found no mention of either, after a certain date, in the letters of Constance, Robert or Emily, which makes it seem likely both died young. Fitzgeorge refers, in a letter to Robert written in his old age, to some friend of their youth who was thrown from his horse and killed, riding back after a visit to their home. The young man, whose name doesn't appear, was alone; and the evening, which was in autumn, was fine though late. Fitzgeorge wonders, and says he will always wonder, what made the horse shy in those empty fields.'

113

Hand in Glove

Jasmine Lodge was favourably set on a residential, prettily-wooded hillside in the south of Ireland, overlooking a river and, still better, the roofs of a lively garrison town. Around 1904, which was the flowering period of the Miss Trevors, girls could not have had a more auspicious home – the neighbourhood spun merrily round the military. Ethel and Elsie, a spirited pair, garnered the full advantage – no ball, hop, picnic, lawn tennis, croquet or boating party was complete without them; in winter, though they could not afford to hunt, they trimly bicycled to all meets, and on frosty evenings, with their guitars, set off to *soirées*, snug inside their cab in their fur-tipped capes.

They possessed an aunt, a Mrs. Varley de Grey, *née* Elysia Trevor, a formerly notable local belle, who, drawn back again in her widowhood to what had been the scene of her early triumphs, occupied a back bedroom in Jasmine Lodge. Mrs. Varley de Grey had had no luck: her splashing match, in its time the talk of two kingdoms, had ended up in disaster – the well-born captain in a cavalry regiment having gone so far as to blow out his brains in India, leaving behind him nothing but her and debts. Mrs. Varley de Grey had returned from India with nothing but seven large trunks crammed with recent finery; and she also had been impaired by shock. This had taken place while Ethel and Elsie, whose father had married late, were still unborn – so it was that, for as long as the girls recalled, their aunt had been the sole drawback to Jasmine Lodge. Their parents had orphaned them, somewhat thought-lessly, by simultaneously dying of scarlet fever when Ethel was just out and Elsie soon to be – they were therefore left lacking a chaperone and, with their gift for putting everything to some use, propped the aunt up in order that she might play that role. Only when her peculiarities became too marked did they feel it necessary to withdraw her: by that time, however, all the surrounding ladies could be said to compete for the honour of taking into society the sought-after Miss Trevors. From then on, no more was seen or heard of Mrs. Varley de Grey. ('Oh, just a trifle unwell, but nothing much!') She remained upstairs, at the back: when the girls were giving one of their little parties, or a couple of officers came to call, the key of her room would be turned in the outer lock.

The girls hung Chinese lanterns from the creepered veranda, and would sit lightly strumming on their guitars. Not less fascinating was their badinage, accompanied by a daring flash of the eyes. They were known as the clever Miss Trevors, not because of any taint of dogmatism or book-learning – no, when a gentleman cried, 'Those girls have brains!' he meant it wholly in admiration – but because of their accomplishments, ingenuity and agility. They took leading parts in theatricals, lent spirit to numbers of drawing-room games, were naughty mimics, and sang duets. Nor did their fingers lag behind their wits – they constructed lampshades, crêpe paper flowers and picturesque hats; and, above all, varied their dresses marvellously – no one could beat them for ideas, nipping, slashing or fitting. Once more allowing nothing to go to waste, they had remodelled the trousseau out of their aunt's trunks, causing sad old tulles and tarlatans, satins and *moiré* taffetas, to appear to have come from Paris only to-day. They re-stitched spangles, pressed ruffles crisp, and revived many a corsage of squashed silk roses. They went somewhat softly about that task, for the trunks were all stored in the attic immediately over the back room.

They wore their clothes well. 'A pin on either of those two would look smart!' declared other girls. All that they were short of was evening gloves – they had two pairs each, which they had been compelled to buy. *What* could have become of Mrs. Varley de Grey's presumably sumptuous numbers of this item, they were unable to fathom, and it was too bad. Had gloves been overlooked in her rush from India? – or, were they here, in that *one* trunk the Trevors could not get at? All other locks had yielded to pulls or pickings, or the sisters found keys to fit them, or they had used the tool-box; but this last stronghold defied them. In that sad little soiled silk sack, always on her person, Mrs. Varley de Grey, they became convinced, hoarded the operative keys, along with some frippery rings and brooches – all true emeralds, pearls and diamonds having been long ago, as they knew, sold. Such contrariety on their aunt's part irked them – meanwhile, gaieties bore hard on their existing gloves. Last thing at nights when they came in, last thing in the evenings before they went out, they would manfully dab away at the fingertips. So, it must be admitted that a long whiff of benzine pursued them as they whirled round the ballroom floor.

They were tall and handsome – nothing so soft as pretty, but in those days it was a vocation to be a handsome girl; many of the best marriages had been made by such. They carried themselves imposingly, had good busts and shoulders, waists firm under the whalebone, and straight backs. Their features were striking, their colouring high; low on their foreheads bounced dark mops of curls. Ethel was, perhaps, the dominant one, but both girls were pronounced to be full of character.

Whom, and still more when, did they mean to marry? They had already seen regiments out and in; for quite a number of years, it began to seem, bets in the neighbourhood had been running high. Sympathetic spy-glasses were trained on the conspicuous gateway to Jasmine Lodge; each new cavalier was noted. The only trouble might be, their promoters claimed, that the clever Trevors were always so surrounded that they had not a moment in which to turn or choose. Or otherwise, could it possibly be that the admiration aroused by Ethel and Elsie, and their now institutional place in the local scene, scared out more tender feeling from the masculine breast? It came to be felt, and perhaps by the girls themselves, that, having lingered so long and so puzzlingly, it was up to them to bring off (like their aunt) a *coup*. Society around this garrison town had long plumed itself upon its romantic record; summer and winter, Cupid shot his darts. Lush scenery, the oblivion of all things else bred by the steamy climate, and perpetual gallivanting – all were conducive. Ethel's and Elsie's names, it could be presumed, were by now murmured wherever the Union Jack flew. Nevertheless, it was time they should decide.

Ethel's decision took place late one spring. She set her cap at the second son of an English marquess. Lord Fred had come on a visit, for the fishing, to a mansion some miles down the river from Jasmine Lodge. He first made his appearance, with the rest of the house party, at one of the more resplendent military balls, and was understood to be a man-about-town. The civilian glint of his pince-nez, at once serene and superb, instantaneously wrought, with his great name, on Ethel's heart. She beheld him, and the assembled audience, with approbation, looked on at the moment so big with fate. The truth, it appeared in a flash, was that Ethel, though so condescending with her charms, had not from the first been destined to love a soldier; and that here, after long attrition, her answer was. Lord Fred was, by all, at once signed over to her. For his part, he responded to her attentions quite gladly, though in a somewhat dazed way. If he did not so often dance with her – indeed, how could he, for she was much besought? – he could at least be perceived to gaze. At a swiftly organised river picnic, the next evening, he by consent fell to Ethel's lot – she had spent the foregoing morning snipping and tacking at a remaining muslin of Mrs. Varley de Grey's, a very fresh forget-me-not-dotted pattern. The muslin did not survive the evening out, for when the moon should have risen, rain poured into the boats. Ethel's good-humoured drollery carried all before it, and Lord Fred wrapped his blazer around her form.

Next day, more rain; and all felt flat. At Jasmine Lodge, the expectant deck chairs had to be hurried in from the garden, and the small close rooms, with their greeneried windows and plantiful bric-à-brac, gave out a stuffy, resentful, indoor smell. The maid was out; Elsie was lying down with a migraine; so it devolved on Ethel to carry up Mrs. Varley de Grey's tea – the invalid set very great store by tea, and her manifestations by door rattlings, sobs and mutters were apt to become disturbing if it did not appear. Ethel, with the not particularly dainty tray, accordingly entered the back room, this afternoon rendered dark by its outlook into a dripping uphill wood. The aunt, her visage draped in a cobweb shawl, was as usual sitting up in bed. *'Aha,'* she at once cried, screwing one eye up and glittering round at Ethel with the other, 'so what's all this in the wind today?'

Ethel, as she lodged the meal on the bed, shrugged her shoulders, saying: 'I'm in a hurry.'

'No doubt you are. The question is, will you get him?'

'Oh, drink your tea!' snapped Ethel, her colour rising.

The old wretch responded by popping a lump of sugar into her cheek, and sucking at it while she fixed her wink on her niece. She then observed: '*I* could tell you a thing or two!'

'We've had enough of *your* fabrications, Auntie.'

'Fabrications!' croaked Mrs. Varley de Grey. 'And who's been the fabricator, I'd like to ask? Who's so nifty with the scissors and needle? Who's been going a-hunting in my clothes?'

'Oh, what a fib!' exclaimed Ethel, turning her eyes up. 'Those old musty miserable bundles of things of yours – would Elsie or I consider laying a finger on them?'

Mrs. Varley de Grey replied, as she sometimes did, by heaving up and throwing the tray at Ethel. Nought, therefore, but cast-off kitchen china nowadays was ever exposed to risk; and the young woman, not trying to gather the debris up, statuesquely, thoughtfully stood with

118

her arms folded, watching tea steam rise from the carpet. Today, the effort required seemed to have been too much for Aunt Elysia, who collapsed on her pillows, faintly blue in the face. 'Rats in the attic,' she muttered. '*I've* heard them, rats in the attic! Now where's my tea?'

'You've had it,' said Ethel, turning to leave the room. However, she paused to study a photograph in a tarnished, elaborate silver frame. 'Really quite an Adonis, poor Uncle Harry. – From the first glance, you say, he never looked back?'

'My lovely tea,' said her aunt, beginning to sob.

As Ethel slowly put down the photograph, her eyes could be seen to calculate, her mouth hardened and a reflective cast came over her brow. Step by step, once more she approached the bed, and, as she did so, altered her tune. She suggested, in a beguiling tone: 'You said you could tell me a thing or two . . . ?'

Time went on; Lord Fred, though forever promising, still failed to come quite within Ethel's grasp. Ground gained one hour seemed to be lost the next – it seemed, for example, that things went better for Ethel in the afternoons, in the open air, than at the dressier evening functions. It was when she swept down on him in full plumage that Lord Fred seemed to contract. Could it be that he feared his passions? – she hardly thought so. Or, did her complexion not light up well? When there was a question of dancing, he came so late that her programme already was black with other names, whereupon he would heave a gallant sigh. When they did take the floor together, he held her so far at arm's length, and with his face turned so far away, that when she wished to address him she had to shout – she told herself this must be the London style, but it piqued her, naturally. Next morning, all would be as it was before, with nobody so completely assiduous as Lord Fred – but, through it all, he still never came to the point. And worse, the days of his visit were running out: he would soon be back in the heart of the London Season.

'Will you ever get him, Ethel, now, do you think?' Elsie asked, with trying solicitude, and no doubt the neighbourhood wondered also.

She conjured up all her fascinations. But was something further needed, to do the trick?

It was now that she began to frequent her aunt.

In that dank little back room looking into the hill, proud Ethel humbled herself, to prise out the secret. Sessions were close and long. Elsie, in mystification outside the door, heard the dotty voice of their relative rising, falling, with, now and then, blood-curdling little knowing laughs. Mrs. Varley de Grey was back in the golden days. Always, though, of a sudden it would break off, drop back into pleas, whimpers and jagged breathing. No doctor, though she constantly asked for one, had for years been allowed to visit Mrs. Varley de Grey — the girls saw no reason for that expense, or for the interference which might follow. Aunt's affliction, they swore, was confined to the head; all she required was quiet, and that she got. Knowing, however, how gossip spreads, they would let no servant near her for more than a minute or two, and then with one of themselves on watch at the door. They had much to bear from the foetid state of her room.

'You don't think you'll kill her, Ethel?' the out-of-it Elsie asked. 'Forever sitting on top of her, as you now do. Can it be healthy, egging her on to talk? What's this at-traction, all of a sudden? — whatever's this which has sprung up between you two? She and you are becoming quite hand-in-glove.'

Elsie merely remarked this, and soon forgot: she had her own fish to fry. It was Ethel who had cause to recall the words — for, the afternoon of the very day they were spoken, Aunt Elysia whizzed off on another track, screamed for what was impossible and, upon being thwarted, went into a seizure unknown before. The worst of it was, at the outset her mind cleared — she pushed her shawl back, reared up her unkempt grey head and looked at Ethel, unblinkingly studied Ethel, with a lucid accumulation of years of hate. 'You fool of a gawk,' she said, and with such contempt! 'Coming running to me to know how to trap a man. Could *you* learn, if it was from Venus herself? Wait till I show you beauty. – Bring down those trunks!'

'Oh, Auntie.'

'Bring them down, I say. I'm about to dress myself up.'

'Oh, but I cannot; they're heavy; I'm single-handed.'

'Heavy? – they came here heavy. But there've been rats in the attic. – *I* saw you, swishing downstairs in my *eau-de-nil*!'

'Oh, you dreamed that!'

'Through the crack of the door. – Let me up, then. Let us go where they are, and look – we shall soon see!' Aunt Elysia threw back the bedclothes and began to get up. 'Let's take a look,' she said, 'at the rats' work.' She set out to totter towards the door.

'Oh, but you're not fit!' Ethel protested.

'And when did a doctor say so?' There was a swaying: Ethel caught her in time and, not gently, lugged her back to the bed – and Ethel's mind the whole of this time was whirling, for tonight was the night upon which all hung. Lord Fred's last local appearance was to be, like his first, at a ball: tomorrow he left for London. So it must be tonight, at this ball, or never! How was it that Ethel felt so strangely, wildly confident of the outcome? It was time to begin on her coiffure, lay out her dress. Oh, tonight she would shine as never before! She flung back the bedclothes over the helpless form, heard a clock strike, and hastily turned to go.

'I will be quits with you,' said the voice behind her.

Ethel, in a kimono, hair half done, was in her own room, in front of the open glove drawer, when Elsie came in – home from a tennis party. Elsie acted oddly; she went at once to the drawer and buried her nose in it. 'Oh, my goodness,' she cried, 'it's all too true, and it's awful!'

'What is?' Ethel carelessly asked.

'Ethel dear, would you ever face it out if I were to tell you a certain rumour I heard today at the party as to Lord Fred?'

Ethel turned from her sister, took up the heated tongs and applied more crimps to her natural curliness. She said: 'Certainly; spit it out.'

'Since childhood, he's recoiled from the breath of benzine. He wilts away when it enters the very room!'

'Who says that's so?'

'He confided it to his hostess, who is now spitefully putting it around the country.'

Ethel bit her lip and put down the tongs, while Elsie sorrowfully concluded: 'and your gloves stink, Ethel, as I'm sure do mine.' Elsie then thought it wiser to slip away.

In a minute more, however, she was back, and this time with a still more peculiar air. She demanded: 'In what state did you leave Auntie? She was sounding so very quiet that I peeped in, and *I* don't care for the looks of her now at all!' Ethel swore, but consented to take a look. She stayed in there in the back room, with Elsie biting her thumb-nail outside the door, for what seemed an ominous length of time — when she did emerge, she looked greenish, but held her head high. The sisters' eyes met. Ethel said, stonily: 'Dozing.'

'You're certain she's *not* . . . ? She *couldn't* ever be — you know?'

'Dozing, I tell you.' Ethel stared Elsie out.

'If she *was* gone,' quavered the frailer sister, 'just think of it — why, we'd never get to the ball! — And a ball that everything hangs on,' she ended up, with a scared but conspiratorial glance at Ethel.

'Reassure yourself. Didn't you hear me say?'

As she spoke Ethel, chiefly from habit, locked her late aunt's door on the outside. The act caused a sort of secret jingle to be heard from inside her fist, and Elsie asked: 'What's that you've got hold of, now?' 'Just a few little keys and trinkets she made me keep,' replied Ethel, disclosing the small bag she had found where she'd looked for it, under the dead one's pillow. 'Scurry on now, Elsie, or you'll never be dressed. Care to make use of my tongs, while they're so splendidly hot?'

Alone at last, Ethel drew in a breath, and, with a gesture of resolution, retied her kimono sash tightly over her corset. She shook the key from the bag and regarded it, murmuring, 'Providential!', then gave a glance upward, towards where the attics were. The late spring sun had set, but an apricot afterglow, not unlike the light cast by a Chinese lantern, crept through the upper storey of Jasmine Lodge. The cessation of all those rustlings, tappings, whimpers and moans from inside Mrs. Varley de Grey's room had set up an unfamiliar, somewhat unnerving hush. Not till a whiff of singeing hair announced that Elsie was well employed did Ethel set out on the quest which held all her hopes. Success was imperative – she *must* have gloves. Gloves, gloves . . . .

Soundlessly, she set foot on the attic stairs.

Under the skylight, she had to suppress a shriek, for a rat – yes, of all things! – leaped at her out of an empty hatbox; and the rodent gave her a wink before it darted away. Now Ethel and Elsie knew for a certain fact that there never *had* been rats in Jasmine Lodge. However, she continued to steel her nerves, and to push her way to the one inviolate trunk.

All Mrs. Varley de Grey's other Indian luggage gaped and yawned at Ethel, void, showing its linings, on end or toppling, forming a barricade around the object of her search – she pushed, pitched and pulled, scowling as the dust flew into her hair. But the last trunk, when it came into view and reach, still had something select and bridal about it: on top, the initials E. V. de G. stared out, quite luminous in a frightening way – for indeed how dusky the attic was! Shadows not only multiplied in the corners but seemed to finger their way up the sloping roof. Silence pierced up through the floor from that room below – and, worst, Ethel had the sensation of being watched by that pair of fixed eyes she had not stayed to close. She glanced this way, that way, backward over her shoulder. But, Lord Fred was at stake! — she knelt down and got to work with the key.

This trunk had two neat brass locks, one left, one right, along the front of the lid. Ethel, after fumbling, opened the first — then, so great was her hurry to know what might be within that she could not wait but slipped her hand in under the lifted corner. She pulled out one pricelessly lacy tip of what must be a bride-veil, and gave a quick laugh — must not this be an omen? She pulled again, but the stuff resisted, almost as though it were being grasped from inside the trunk — she let go, and either her eyes deceived her or the lace began to be drawn back slowly, in again, inch by inch. What was odder was, that the spotless finger-tip of a white kid glove appeared for a moment, as though exploring its way out, then withdrew.

Ethel's heart stood still — but she turned to the other lock. Was a giddy attack overcoming her? — for, as she gazed, the entire lid of the trunk seemed to bulge upward, heave and strain, so that the E. V. de G. upon it rippled.

Untouched by the key in her trembling hand, the second lock tore itself open.

She recoiled, while the lid slowly rose — of its own accord.

She should have fled. But oh, how she craved what lay there exposed! — layer upon layer, wrapped in transparent paper, of elbow-length, magnolia-pure white gloves, bedded on the inert folds of the veil. 'Lord Fred,' thought Ethel, 'Now you're within my grasp!'

That was her last thought, nor was the grasp to be hers. Down on her knees again, breathless with lust and joy, Ethel flung herself forward on to that sea of kid, scrabbling and seizing. The glove she had seen before was now, however, readier for its purpose. At first it merely pounced after Ethel's fingers, as though making mock of their greedy course; but the hand within it was all the time filling out. . . . With one snowy flash through the dusk, the glove clutched Ethel's front hair, tangled itself in her black curls and dragged her head down. She began to choke among the sachets and tissue – then the glove let go, hurled her back, and made its leap at her throat.

It was a marvel that anything so dainty should be so strong. So great, so convulsive was the swell of the force that, during the strangling of Ethel, the seams of the glove split.

In any case, the glove would have been too small for her.

The shrieks of Elsie, upon the attic threshold, began only when all other sounds had died down. . . . The ultimate spark of the once-famous cleverness of the Miss Trevors appeared in Elsie's extrication of herself from this awkward mess – for, who was to credit how Ethel came by her end? The sisters' reputation for warmth of heart was to stand the survivor in good stead – for, could those affections nursed in Jasmine Lodge, extending so freely even to the unwell aunt, have culminated in Elsie's setting on Ethel? No. In the end, the matter was hushed up – which is to say, is still talked about even now. Ethel Trevor and Mrs. Varley de Grey were interred in the same grave, as everyone understood that they would have wished. What conversation took place under the earth, one does not know.

A Day in the Dark

Coming into Moher over the bridge, you may see a terrace of houses by the river. They are to the left of the bridge, below it. Their narrow height and faded air of importance make them seem to mark the approach to some larger town. The six dwellings unite into one frontage, colour-washed apricot years ago. They face north. Their lower sash windows, front steps and fanlit front doors are screened by lime trees, making for privacy. There are area railings. Between them and the water runs a road with a parapet, which comes to its end opposite the last house.

On the other side of the bridge picturesquely rises a ruined castle ˙– more likely to catch the tourist's eye. Woods, from which the river emerges, go back deeply behind the ruin: on clear days there is a backdrop of Irish-blue mountains. Otherwise Moher has little to show. The little place prospers – a market town with a square, on a main road. The hotel is ample, cheerful, and does business. Moreover Moher is, and has been for ages, a milling town. Obsolete stone buildings follow you some way along the river valley as, having passed through Moher, you pursue your road. The flour-white modern mills, elsewhere, hum.

Round the square, shops and pubs are of many colours – in the main Moher looks like a chalk drawing. Not so the valley with its elusive lights.

You *could*, I can see, overlook my terrace of houses – because of the castle, indifference or haste. I only do not because I am looking out for them. For in No. 4 lived Miss Banderry.

She was the last of a former milling family – last, that is, but for the widowed niece, her pensioner. She owned the terrace, drew rents also from property in another part of the town, and had acquired, some miles out of Moher, a profitable farm which she'd put to management. Had control of the family mills been hers, they would not have been parted with — as it was, she had had to contend with a hopeless brother: he it was who had ended by selling out. Her demand for her share of the money left him unable to meet personal debts: he was found hanged from one of the old mill crossbeams. Miss Banderry lived in retirement, the more thought of for being seldom seen — now and then she would summon a Ford hackney and drive to her farm in it, without warning. My uncle, whose land adjoined on hers, had dealings with her, in the main friendly — which was how they first fell into talk. She, a formidable reader, took to sending him serious magazines, reviews, pamphlets and so on, with marked passages on which she would be dying to hear his views. This was her way of harrying him. For my uncle, a winning, versatile and when necessary inventive talker, fundamentally hated to tax his brain. He took to evading meetings with her as far as possible.

So much I knew when I rang her doorbell.

It was July, a sunless warm afternoon, dead still. The terrace was heavy with limes in flower. Above, through the branches, appeared the bridge with idlers who leaned on the balustrade spying down upon me, or so I thought. I felt marked by visiting this place — I was fifteen, and my every sensation was acute in a way I recall, yet cannot recall. All six houses were locked in childless silence. From under the parapet came languidly the mesmeric sound of the weir, and, from a window over my head, the wiry hopping of a bird in a cage. From the shabby other doors of the terrace, No. 4's stood out, handsomely though sombrely painted red. It opened.

I came to return a copy of *Blackwoods*. Also I carried a bunch of ungainly roses from my uncle's garden, and a request that he might borrow the thistle cutter from Miss Banderry's farm for use on his land. One rose moulted petals on to her doorstep, then on to the linoleum in the hall. 'Goodness!' complained the niece, who had let me in. 'Those didn't travel well. Overblown, aren't they!' (I thought that applied to her.) 'And I'll bet,' she said, '*he* never sent those!' She was not in her aunt's confidence, being treated more or less like a slave. Timed (they said) when she went errands into the town — she dare not stay talking, dare not so much as look into the hotel bar while the fun was on. For a woman said to be forty, this sounded mortifying. Widowed Nan, ready to be handsome, wore a cheated ravenous look. It was understood she would come into the money when the aunt died: she must contain herself till then. As for me — how dared she speak of my uncle with her bad breath?

Naturally he *had* never thought of the roses. He had commissioned me to be gallant for him any way I chose, and I would not do too badly with these, I'd thought, as I unstrangled them from the convolvulus in the flowerbed. They would need not only to flatter but to propitiate, for this copy of *Blackwoods* I brought back had buttery thumb-marks on its margins and on its cover a blistered circle where my uncle must have stood down his glass. 'She'll be mad,' he prophesied. 'Better say it was you.' So I sacrificed a hair ribbon to tie the roses. It rejoiced me to stand between him and trouble.

'Auntie's resting,' the niece warned me, and put me to wait. The narrow parlour looked out through thick lace on to the terrace, which was reflected in a looking-glass at the far end. Ugly though I could see honourable furniture, mahogany, had been crowded in. In the middle, a circular table wore a chenille cloth. This room felt respected though seldom entered — however, it was peopled in one way: generations of oil-painted portraits hung round the walls, photographs overflowed from bracket and ledge even on to the centre table. I was faced, wherever I turned, by one or another member of the family which could only be the vanished Banderrys. There was a marble clock, but it had stopped.

Footsteps halted heavily over the ceiling, but that was all for I don't know how long. I began to wonder what those Banderrys saw — lodging the magazine and roses on the table, I went to inspect myself in the glass. A tall girl in a sketchy cotton dress. Arms thin, no sign yet of a figure. Hair forward over the shoulders in two plaits, like, said my uncle, a Red Indian maiden's. Barbie was my name.

In memory, the moment before often outlives the awaited moment. I recollect waiting for Miss Banderry — then, nothing till she was with me in the room. I got over our handshake without feeling. On to the massiveness of her bust was pinned a diamond-studded enamelled watch, depending from an enamelled bow: there was a tiny glitter as she drew breath. — 'So he sent *you*, did he?' She sat down, the better to take a look at me. Her apart knees stretched the skirt of her dress. Her choleric colouring and eyeballs made her appear angry, as against which she favoured me with a racy indulgent smile, to counteract the impression she knew she gave.

'I hear wonders of you,' said she, dealing the lie to me like a card.

She sat in reach of the table. 'My bouquet, eh?' She grasped the bundle of roses, thorns and all, and took a long voluptuous sniff at them, as though deceiving herself as to their origin — showing me she knew how to play the game, if I didn't — then shoved back the roses among the photographs and turned her eyes on the magazine, sharply. 'I'm sorry, I — ' I began. In vain. All she gave was a rumbling chuckle — she held up to me the copy of *Blackwoods* open at the page with the most thumbmarks. 'I'd know *those* anywhere!' She scrutinised the print for a line or two. 'Did he make head or tail of it?'

'He told me to tell you, he enjoyed it.' (I saw my uncle dallying, stuffing himself with the buttered toast.) 'With his best thanks.'

'You're a little echo,' she said, not discontentedly.

I stared her out.

'Never mind,' she said. 'He's a handsome fellow.'

I shifted my feet. She gave me a look.

She observed: 'It's a pity to read at table.'

'He hasn't much other time, Miss Banderry.'

'Still, it's a poor compliment to you!'

She stung me into remarking: 'He doesn't often.'

'Oh, I'm sure you're a great companion for him!'

It was as though she saw me casting myself down by my
uncle's chair when he'd left the room, or watching the las-
situde of his hand hanging caressing a dog's ear. With him
I felt the tender bond of sex. Seven, eight weeks with him
under his roof, among the copper beeches from spring to
summer turning from pink to purple, and I was in love
with him. Such things happen, I suppose. He was my
mother's brother, but I had not known him when I was a
child. Of his manhood I had had no warning. Naturally
growing into love I was, like the grass growing into hay
on his uncut lawns. There was not a danger till she spoke.

'He's glad of company now and then,' I said as stupidly
as I could.

She plucked a petal from her black serge skirt.

'Well,' she said, 'thank him for the thanks. And you for
the nice little pleasure of this visit. — Then, there's nothing
else?'

'My uncle wants — ' I began.

'You don't surprise me,' said Miss Banderry. 'Well,
come on out with it. What this time?'

'If he could once more borrow the thistle cutter . . . ?'

' "Once more"! And what will he be looking to do next
year? Get his own mended? I suppose he'd hardly go to
that length.'

His own, I knew, had been sold for scrap. He was
sometimes looking for ready money. I said nothing.

'Looking to me to keep him out of jail?' (Law forbids
one to suffer the growth of thistles.) 'Time after time, it's
the same story. It so happens, I haven't mine cut yet!'

'He'd be glad to lend you his jennet back, he says, to
draw the cutter for you.'

'*That* brute! There'd be nothing for me to cut if it wasn't

130

for what blows in off his dirty land.' With the flat of her fingers she pressed one eyeball, then the other, back into her head. She confessed, all at once almost plaintively: 'I don't care to have machinery leave my farm.'

'Very well,' I said haughtily, 'I'll tell him.'

She leaned back, rubbed his palms on her thighs. 'No, wait — this you may tell my lord. Tell him I'm not sure, but I'll think it over. There might be a favourable answer, there might not. If my lord would like to know which, let him come himself. — That's a sweet little dress of yours,' she went on, examining me inside it, 'but it's skimpy. He should do better than hide behind *those* skirts!'

'I don't know what you mean, Miss Banderry.'

'He'd know.'

'Today, my uncle *was* busy.'

'I'm sure he was. Busy day after day. In my life, I've known only one other man anything like so busy as your uncle. And shall I tell you who that was? My poor brother.'

After all these years, that terrace focuses dread. I mislike any terrace facing a river. I suppose I would rather look upon it itself (as I must, whenever I cross that bridge) than be reminded of it by harmless others. True, only one house in it was Miss Banderry's, but the rest belong to her by complicity. An indelible stain is on that monotony — the extinct pink frontage, the road leading to nothing but those six doors which the lime trees, flower as they may, exist for nothing but to shelter. The monotony of the weir and the hopping bird. Within that terrace I was in one room only, and only once.

My conversation with Miss Banderry did not end where I leave off recording it. But at that point memory is torn across, as might be an intolerable page. The other half is missing. For that reason my portrait of her would be incomplete if it *were* a portrait. She could be novelist's material, I daresay — indeed novels, particularly the French and Irish (for Ireland in some ways resembles France) are

131

full of prototypes of her: oversized women insulated in little provincial towns. Literature, once one knows it, drains away some of the shockingness out of life. But when I met her I was unread, my susceptibilities were virgin. I refuse to fill in her outline retrospectively: I show you only what I saw at the time. Not what she was, but what she did to me.

Her amorous hostility to my uncle – or was it hostility making use of a farce? – unsheathed itself when she likened him to the brother she drove to death.

When I speak of dread I mean dread, not guilt. That afternoon, I went to Miss Banderry's for my uncle's sake, in his place. It could be said, my gathering of foreboding had to do with my relation with him – yet in that there was no guilt anywhere, I could swear! I swear we did each other no harm. I think he was held that summer, as I was, by the sense that this was a summer like no other and which could never again be. Soon I must grow up, he must grow old. Meanwhile we played house together on the margin of a passion which was impossible. My longing was for him, not for an embrace – as for him, he was glad of companionship, as I'd truly told her. He was a man tired by a lonely house till I joined him – a schoolgirl between schools. All thought well of his hospitality to me. Convention was our safeguard: could one have stronger?

I left No. 4 with ceremony. I was offered raspberry cordial. Nan bore in the tray with the thimble glasses – educated by going visiting with my uncle, I knew refusal would mark a breach. When the glasses were emptied, Nan conducted me out of the presence, to the hall door – she and I stopped aimlessly on the steps. Across the river throve the vast new mills, unabashed, and cars swished across the tree-ridden bridge. The niece showed a reluctance to go in again – I think the bird above must have been hers. She glanced behind her, then conspiratorially at me. 'So now you'll be going to the hotel?'

'No. Why?'

' "Why?" ' she jibed. 'Isn't he waiting for you? Anyway, that's where he is: in there. The car's outside.'

I said: 'But I'm taking the bus home.'

'Now, why ever?'

'I said I would take the bus. I came in that way.'

'You're mad. What, with his car in the square?'

All I could say was: 'When?'

'I slipped out just now,' said the niece, 'since you want to know. To a shop, only. While you were chatting with Auntie.' She laughed, perhaps at her life, and impatiently gave me a push away. 'Get on — wherever you're going to! Anybody would think you'd had bad news!'

Not till I was almost on the bridge did I hear No. 4's door shut.

I leaned on the balustrade, at the castle side. The river, coming towards me out of the distances of woods, washed the bastions and carried a paper boat — this, travelling at uncertain speed on the current, listed as it vanished under the bridge. I had not the heart to wonder how it would fare. Weeks ago, when first I came to my uncle's, here we had lingered, elbow to elbow, looking up-river through the green-hazed spring hush at the far off swan's nest, now deserted. Next I raised my eyes to the splendid battlements, kissed by the sky where they were broken.

From the bridge to the town rises a slow hill — shops and places of business come down to meet you, converting the road into a street. There are lamp posts, signboards, yard gates pasted with layers of bills, and you tread pavement. That day the approach to Moher, even the crimson valerian on stone walls, was filmed by imponderable white dust as though the flourbags had been shaken. To me, this was the pallor of suspense. An all but empty theatre was the square, which, when I entered it at a corner, paused between afternoon and evening. In the middle were parked cars, looking forgotten — my uncle's was nearest the hotel.

The hotel, glossy with green creeper, accounted for one end of the square. A cream porch, figuring the name in

133

gold, framed the doorway — though I kept my back to that I expected at any moment to hear a shout as I searched for the independence of my bus. But where *that* should have waited, I found nothing. Nothing, at this bus end of the square, but a drip of grease on dust and a torn ticket. 'She's gone out, if that's what you're looking for,' said a bystander. So there it went, carrying passengers I was not among to the scenes of safety, and away from me every hope of solitude. Out of reach was the savingness of a house empty. Out of reach, the windows down to the ground open upon the purple beeches and lazy hay, the dear weather of those rooms in and out of which flew butterflies, my cushions on the floor, my blue striped tea mug. Out of reach, the whole of the lenient meaning of my uncle's house, which most filled it when he was not there ... I did not want to be bothered with him, I think.

'She went out on time today, more's the pity.'

Down hung my hair in two weighted ropes as I turned away.

Moher square is oblong. Down its length, on the two sides, people started to come to the shop doors in order to look at me in amazement. They knew who I was and where he was: what should *I* be wanting to catch the bus for? They speculated. As though a sandal chafed me I bent down, spent some time loosening the strap. Then, as though I had never had any other thought, I started in the direction of the hotel.

At the same time, my uncle appeared in the porch. He tossed a cigarette away, put the hand in a pocket and stood there under the gold lettering. He was not a lord, only a landowner. Facing Moher, he was all carriage and colouring: he wore his life like he wore his coat — though, now he was finished with the hotel, a light hint of melancholy settled down on him. He was not looking for me until he saw me.

We met at his car. He asked: 'How was she, the old terror?'

'I don't know.'

134

'She didn't eat you?'

'No,' I said, shaking my head.

'Or send me another magazine?'

'No. Not this time.'

'Thank God.'

He opened the car door and touched my elbow, reminding me to get in.